FUREY'S WAR

Other books by TW Lawless:

HOMECOUNTRY

THORNYDEVILS

BLURLINE

DARK WATER

FLAMEKEEPER

Other books by Kay Bell:

THE LORNESLEIGH LEGACY

ELLA'S SECRET FAMILY RECIPES

THE AMERICAN GOVERNESS

FUREY'S WAR

T.W. Lawless & Kay Bell

CAMPANILE
PUBLISHING

Published by Campanile Publishing
www.twlawless.com

The views of the characters and terms used in this book do not reflect those of the authors. They are, however, consistent with the time in which this book is set.

A National Library of Australia Cataloguing-in-Publication entry has been created for this title.

ISBN 978-0-6450991-9-5 (pbk)

ISBN 978-0-6450991-8-8 (ebook)

Cover design by Golden Orb Creative: www.goldenorbcreative.com
Cover image by Vladm used under licence from Shutterstock.com
(photo ID: 1878120166).

Text design and production (print and ebook) by Golden Orb Creative.

Edited by Linda Nix AE of Golden Orb Creative.

PROLOGUE

1942

The fresh blood next to the chinky apple tree attracts a pair of crows.

They perch in a tall paperbark and caw at the dawn. Once the creek mist settles, a mound of leaves catches their attention. Now, there's nothing strange about such a mound in the bush, but this one's out of place: it's a little too neat, with too little foliage around it and too much heaped over it.

The first bird glides down and follows the blood with a string of hops. It climbs on top of the leaves, tosses them off and scrapes away the soil with its beak. It uncovers a bundle no bigger than a rabbit, but it's wedged under a rock, so the bird pecks and tears at it for a while, and then flutters off.

The second bird spots something entirely different in the discarded vegetation, and swoops down. In the end it too flies away, but the fine silver chain with its swinging locket slides from its grip; the necklace rides the breeze back to the ground, and is lost in the undergrowth.

CHAPTER ONE

Nursing Home, 1993

She sits on the arm of my recliner, yelling into my ear until I turn my head and look. There's boredom in her eyes; she's imagining herself somewhere else and I'm the only thing stopping her from getting there.

She twists around and starts up again. She's shaking me too, though I barely feel it.

'Mr Furey… Mr Furey…'

I know who I bloody well am, and I'm not deaf. Read the bloody care plan.

Any moment now she'll make my ear wax pop out.

She's not my usual girl; I get the feeling that she doesn't know a thing about me. From the look of her, she's a lazy bugger. She's all a bit crumpled, like she picked her uniform up off the floor this morning, put it on and came to work.

'Mr Furey,' she continues, 'you were having a terrible nightmare.'

I admit a moment ago there were pictures in my head I'd sooner not see: flashbacks, I suppose you'd call them. Like autumn mists they come, and then they go again once the morning sun breaks through. If it were up to me, there'd be no more autumns and no more mornings, and the nightmares would be gone for good.

Until she woke me, I didn't even realise I was asleep. I try to explain it to her and she frowns.

The problem is, whenever I try to speak these days, all that happens is my tongue scrapes across my dentures. My mouth wobbles, but no words come out and when I do make a sound, well, to be honest, it's a bit like a fart. All those years of talking without a second thought, and now the best that I can do, after a big effort, is pass wind and dribble. And it's been like that for the last five years.

So, I put my hand on hers and squeeze.

She flinches. 'Not so hard, Mr Furey!' She tries to pull her hand away.

Her face is suddenly as cloudy as a stormy day, and it makes her look stupid. I think about giving her hand another little squeeze, but I change my mind and slowly release her hand. I bang my fist on the bedside table instead. Then I point to my mouth. There I am, caught in the mirror opposite me, my crooked finger raised up to my crooked mouth, which these days is located somewhere near the bottom of my crooked face. It's enough to frighten the birds. Did I mention that I was handsome once? I was so handsome that I caught the eye of the prettiest girl in town. What a dapper couple we made, Grace and me.

And now I can't bear to look at my face in the mirror: I'd spit at the mirror, if I could.

Hard to spit when you've had a stroke.

I shouldn't complain, it's really not as bad as all that. Except that I can't walk or talk, I'm pretty good. And I can't control the waterworks as well as I used to. But I'm still right in the head, you know. So what, if I pee myself from time to time? There's nothing wrong with my mind. In my head, I'm still as sharp as a stockman's pocket knife.

I can tell I've broken through to the girl at last. She softens and puts her arm around me. I try to tell her it's all right, but the effort makes me cry. I know that, because I can feel the tears running down my face. I'd give all of my tomorrows and everything I own just to be able to walk and talk again. Then I realise I don't have much of anything left to give, anyway.

'I'm sorry, I know you can't talk properly, Mr Furey,' she says sympathetically as she grabs a tissue to wipe away my tears. 'It must be hard for you.'

So, I instantly feel sad for her. I read her name tag and try to mouth her name. Tanya. It comes out like *Bhah ba*.

Suddenly, her face lights up. 'Since you're awake, I want to be the first to tell you what the boss has planned for you.'

Now she's beaming like a headlight. What is she talking about? They're going to send me home to die? That'd be a little hard to do, since my mongrel family sold my home after they dropped me off here. Reckon the ink on the contract was still wet when they slammed the door behind me. I can still feel the breeze on my back. The bastards. Sold my property and now they hardly ever visit me.

'It's about your...'

Before she can finish, there's a knock at my door. We both look over. It's the boss of the nursing home, Ben Harrison, although I prefer to call him Shifty. *Shifty Harrison.* I'd call him that to his polished face, if I could only say the bloody words. He's a bloody show-pony. I've seen his kind before. He's a flashy bastard, just like a politician. Thinks he's a corporate boss.

Shifty Harrison dresses in expensive suits and drives one of those German BMW cars. He parades around like a bloody peacock whenever he's out of his office. Which isn't often. I reckon he's in there most of the time with the door shut, giving the secretary a good old-fashioned love-up on his desk.

Shifty pretends to like all us old buggers, but all he sees are dollars signs hanging over our heads. And then he's always thinking about how he can skim more of that his way. As sure as a morning piss, he's diddling the books. I can tell. Just because I had a stroke doesn't mean I've lost my bloody marbles. And I certainly haven't lost my copper's intuition. Yep, I'm still as sharp as a master mason's chisel. The thing is, I never wanted to stop being a copper, and I'd still be a copper now, except that the big-wigs in the city forced me to retire. But at least I managed to hang in there until I was sixty-five.

I've seen and heard enough around here to fuel an investigation. The home's been going downhill big time since he's been the boss: the food isn't fit for a cattle dog, and the carers are untrained and overworked. Shifty Harrison is all about that holy dollar. I could have cooked his goose well and truly, if only I could have gotten out of this chair and had a good snoop around.

So, Shifty's now standing in the middle of my room and the only thing going through my mind is how to get him to leave.

'Mr Furey,' he says, 'how good to see you,' his voice as oily as a car salesman's.

I know the bastard couldn't care less if I died. I'm surprised he even knows my name. Given half a chance, he'd have this room rented out before my still-warm body was loaded into the hearse.

He comes closer and bends over me, his eyes glued on me in the same way that a vet with a syringe in one hand might look at a sick dog. If he goes to pat me on the bloody head, I'll throw my cup of tea at him. Or I'll grab his balls and squeeze the life out of them. Still got strength in my fingers, thank the Lord.

He drags a chair and sits so close to me that I can smell his after-shave. He smells like a bloody woman. He places his hand on mine and holds it. Soft. Not a man's hand. His hands haven't seen any hard work. I try to pull back but he hangs on.

'We have a big party planned for you tomorrow,' Shifty says.

Even with my twisted face, I must still look confused. I grunt as loudly as I can.

'Did you forget, Mr Furey?' He grins at me and then looks over at the carer for support.

'When I walked into his room, he was having another of those nightmares the RN warned me about. At the handover this morning, the nurse said Mr Furey seemed more confused than normal. He forgot where he was yesterday. Tried to go into Myra Little's room.'

The girl's an idiot. Tanya relates this as if I'm not really here, but I'm used to that. When you're old, you become deaf and invisible. Either they yell at you, or it's like you're not in the room.

But I am here.

What do you bloody mean, I'm more confused? Aren't you allowed to forget anything when you get to my age? Is it a bloody crime?

I can remember pretty much everything about my life, and that's ninety-nine percent of the problem. So what if I've forgotten what I ate or when I last had a shit, or where my room is? Of course I forget where I am. I want to forget this place. I try very hard to forget I'm here, because I don't want to be here. I want to go home. I always thought I'd die at home, in my warm bed, next to Gracie. I never figured on ending my days in a lifeless, money-sucking shithole.

'Do you know how old you are tomorrow, Mr Furey?' Shifty asks brightly.

It's like he's talking to a child. He's just as much an idiot as Tanya.

There's no chance for sarcasm, so the best I can do is nod, as I roll my eyes for the umpteenth time today.

'So you know it's your birthday tomorrow?'

I nod again. I grab a pen and paper and write my birth date on it. I add where I was born for good measure.

'So you know it's your one hundredth birthday, Mr Furey?'

I grunt again and write. I'm so pissed off that my hand shakes. I give the sheet to Shifty, but he can't read my scrawl. He hands it to Tanya, who reads it to herself, mouthing every syllable. Finally, she makes sense of what I have written. I snigger. Her hand flies up to cover her mouth. She can't stop giggling. I begin to like her better.

My kind of sheila.

Shifty wants in on the joke. 'Tell me what he's written.'

'What…do…you…think…I…am? A…flicking…idiot?' Tanya reads out my words slowly.

It's clear that she's struggling to read my plain English, but Shifty gets the gist. He turns crimson, fishing for a response he simply can't seem to hook. At last, he's lost for words. I've managed to shut the smartarse bastard up.

'Well, Mr Furey,' he stammers at last. 'I came here to tell you in good faith that we are putting on a celebration for your birthday in the dining room at twelve tomorrow. It's a big deal and we've spared no expense. You're the star of the show, so you have to be there.'

I wish he'd run it by me first. I'd have much preferred to have gone to the pub with a few mates. But then again, maybe not. Truth is, most of them are already dead.

'The mayor, his wife, the president of the RSL and the local Member of Parliament are coming just to see you. The mayor will be reading out a message from the Queen. How great is that?'

They're not coming to see me, you fool, they're coming to be seen with me. There's a big difference.

I like the Queen, but as for the rest of them… That Chinless Charlie is about as switched on as blown light bulb. I respect and admire the Queen, right enough. I must do; after all, I fought for her grandfather, the King and the Empire, in the First World War.

'Your family will be here. Val Burgess and her husband will entertain everyone. How lovely is that? The television will be here, too. You'll be on the news, Mr Furey. The cook has baked a cake, of course, big enough for all one hundred candles. How do you like that?'

I roll my eyes. How did I get to be this old and still have to put up with so much crap? As for the cook making a cake… I call him the dingo baiter. He can't cook a sausage.

I mumble disapprovingly. It's wonderful to know that no one cares about what I want. I've lived the hundred years, so why the heck would anyone let me have a say as to who I want to have at my birthday? Well, I don't even want to celebrate it. And if I did, I wouldn't invite any of those so-called dignitaries. They're all useless, arrogant bastards, as far as I can see.

So, why would I want to celebrate another bloody birthday, let alone the fact that I've lived through a hundred of them? The only thing they'll be celebrating tomorrow is my successful inability to die. Birthdays are just an annual reminder that I'm still alive, and everyone I loved isn't. Look at me. There's not much to crow over, and most of the people who are still here with me are in even worse shape. But you know, I've got to be getting close, by now. Can't be too many bloody birthdays left. I sigh and Shifty looks pretty happy, like he realises that he's worn me down.

Let's just get it over and done with.

I'd give anything to see my wife again. I know I'll meet up with Gracie in the great beyond, and won't that be wonderful? I know she'll be waiting for me on the other side. Probably with a hot cup of tea and a nice corned beef sandwich.

After Shifty and Tanya leave my room, I've only just stretched out on my bed when I get another visitor. The door creaks open and I'm thinking that Shifty Harrison's come back for round two and to check if I'm still breathing, when, blow me down, if it isn't my old mate Vivian Morley! He limps in and sits in the spare armchair next to me, smiling so hard that his dentures nearly fall out. I'm pleased to see him. He's a breath of fresh air in this stale old place.

I ask him what he's doing here and he doesn't answer straight-away. Last time I saw Viv was at the Wangamba RSL, Remembrance Day, 1978. I was remembering sixty years since the end of the Great War, and after his fifth round of drinks, he wasn't remembering much of anything.

So, Viv pulls up a chair and asks me about the war. I'm thinking about the trenches when he says that he means to ask me about the other war: the Second World War. I'm about to ask him why, when he leaves the room to take a piss. His interest in the subject's got me thinking, though, about the first day of the 'friendly' invasion.

By the time he returns, it's 1942 and I'm already back home.

CHAPTER TWO

Wangamba, 1942

I reckon the whole town of Wangamba has turned out to see the Yanks arrive. I got the call. They're coming today in a convoy from Townsville, and it was all supposed to be hush-hush. All around me, people are hopping from foot to foot.

So much for secrecy.

Just two days ago, the police commissioner down in Brisbane gave me and my two constables the order to direct them through the town. Not much time to get ready, but then I guess they didn't want word of it getting back to the Japs.

'Now,' said the commissioner, 'we don't want our American allies getting lost in the scrub and dying of thirst, do we, Jack?'

As if he needed to tell me that.

So here I am, standing in the middle of the intersection of Jennings Street—the main street—and Queen Street, on a sweltering hot day, waiting for the Americans to arrive. Crowds have built up all along the route, three deep in some places. There hasn't been a gathering like this since the victory parade after the Great War. I think the attendance was probably bigger in 1919, but that's likely because more people lived in the town back then. Since then, people have been trickling out of Wangamba like piss out of an old man's prostate. We have more feral goats than people living here these days.

I've been trying to work out how the locals found out about their arrival. It's not as if someone placed an advertisement in *The North Star.* I was instructed to tell Mayor Jessop, but no one else, and I never told another soul, not even my Gracie. Even my constables never knew until this morning. Old 'Flapping Gums' Jessop would have to be the source of the leak. He wouldn't have been able to help himself. It'd be just like him to tell anyone who'd listen, big-noting himself, like he's got the inside-running and everyone else is on the outer. Thinks himself a bloody toff. He has big tickets on himself, that bloke.

There are only around a thousand people in Wangamba, including the Aborigines, and every one of them's here: man, woman, child and stray dog. But not the goats. The goats aren't hanging around the streets today. I reckon it must be too noisy for them. And they're too smart to line up just to watch the Americans drive past.

The local Abos are standing in a group by themselves, not far from where I am now. They don't like mixing much with the whites, and vice versa. Nobody seems bothered. It's sort of the natural order of things, I suppose.

Even old Harry Jacka's turned up. He usually lives in a hut in the scrub and has nothing to do with people. Still, here he is, wearing his best gladrags, waiting for the Yanks to file past. No one is standing too close to him, though. I don't think Harry has had a bath since his mother stopped giving him one. He's a hundred yards away from me, and he's still on the nose. I've smelled some pretty bad things in my time—trench foot and mustard gas—yet the slightest whiff of Harry Jacka can really turn a stomach. Right now, it's nearly as bad as being downwind of a bloated cow lying dead in a dam.

At the top of the road, the mayor and his mob of dignitaries stand on a stage bedecked with Australian and American flags and a banner with *Welcome to Our Town* written on it. They're all dressed up like pox doctor's clerks and standing around like shags on a rock. Below them our local brass band's ready to blow out a tune. They usually sound like howling dogs. They begin warming up, and today, for a change, it sounds a lot like someone's strangling a cat.

Out the front of the hospital, they've wheeled some of the patients just so they can get a bit of a view. Some of them don't look long for the world, but they all want to see the Yanks before they kick the bucket. Can't understand the attraction, to be honest with you. I figure they'll be pretty much like any other bloke in uniform, but it seems to me the town's expecting Clark Gable and Fred Astaire to stroll past. I reckon that they think it'll be like Hollywood's coming to town. Wangamba's taken the Yanks so far up the mountain, it's going to be one hell of a long way for them to fall.

Now, don't get me wrong, it's not like it's all bad news. Everyone's ecstatic that the Yanks have joined the war. The Old Country retreated back to Europe after the fall of Singapore, and all our best troops are caught up in the Middle East. For a while now, we've been on our own, and it's been a bit of a bloody worry. There are only seven million of us. We need the Yanks like sheep need water from a dam on a hot day. We might be the best soldiers in the world but we'd be buggered without them, I'll give you that one for free.

I've heard a rumour that we'll be building a secret airfield and barracks out by the river, on the other side of town. Once we've done our bit, the Americans will set up the airfield there, and supply the base. Amazing what you learn when you're in my job. From what I recall, soldiers just love to spend their pay, so their presence should bring in a few quid. In fact, it could be the biggest boom around here since the gold rush. Yep, since the gold ran out, it's been pretty slim pickings. The only things that have stopped Wangamba turning into a ghost town are the cattle stations.

So, here I am, wearing my best uniform today, and Gracie's polished my boots and even the brass on my buttons and on my buckle. She's a good woman, my missus. She insisted I wear my medals, even though I wasn't keen. It's a bit much, don't you think? I feel like a bit of a lair really. I'm not one for showing off.

'You're a fair dinkum war hero, Jack Furey,' she said, 'so don't you hide it. You wear your medals with pride.'

I've learned over the years that when your wife insists you do something, well, you're better off just going along with her: nod your head, hang on and say nothing.

My medals are shining so bright in the sun, that they're just about blinding me.

It seems like there's thunder over the horizon, so loud it makes me look up at the sky. There's not a cloud in sight. I listen for a while, but the noise doesn't go away. I figure it's got to be the rumble of the convoy. It must have reached the outskirts of town. By the sound of it, there are a lot of vehicles headed this way, and I can feel the vibration all the way up my legs. I'm eager to get it all over and done with, go back to the station and have a nice cup of tea. Then a thought forces itself into my mind: what if it's not the Americans at all? I say a silent prayer that it's not the Japs. Just in case.

Whoever it is, it's time to look sharp, Jack Furey.

I adjust my uniform and give my hat a tug, and then I make a hand signal to the constable a hundred yards away. All down the street, the crowd's already cheering. Some of the bystanders push forward, a few even stepping onto the roadway, but I yell at them to get back onto the footpath, quick-smart. People in this town always listen to what a copper tells them. Not too many ratbags or hooligans. Most of them are law-abiding citizens, and the ones who aren't get a swift police escort out of town.

The convoy's getting nearer. The sound is deafening; like a freight train at close quarters. Everyone's heads are turned in the same direction, but all I can see is a huge swirl of bulldust in the distance. It's far bigger than a willy-willy. Hope the Yanks weren't expecting a bitumen highway with roadside stops, or they'll be sorely disappointed. The McEwan Pothole-Way is nothing more than a glorified goat track. No bitumen on any of the roads around here, I'm afraid. I bet the poor buggers are wondering why they're even in this God-forsaken joint.

Just ahead of the rolling cloud is a speeding Willy's Jeep, going hell-for-leather. It's exceeding the speed limit, by a long way.

Not starting with a good impression, you blokes.

Sitting in the Jeep are two men in dusty khakis, helmets tight on their heads. I can only just make out the initials, MP, on their shirt-sleeves, once they get closer. It looks like they're the forward scouts, coming to check out the locals and make sure we're not hostile. The buggers better slow down right now. But my immediate concern isn't their speed, it's that they're driving on the wrong side of the road.

We drive on the left here, boys. On the bloody left.

Luckily there aren't a lot of cars driving around right at the moment. In fact, there aren't any. First thing I'm going to have to do, is explain the road rules to them. Didn't anyone tell these Yanks anything? It all falls to me, I suppose. So muggins me walks to the middle of the road, holds up my hand and signals for them to stop. Meanwhile, the Jeep keeps screaming towards me, and I can't see them slowing down. They're still hurtling along, and they're still on the wrong side of the road. They're getting closer: too close. I'm staring them down, waiting for one of us to draw back.

Just as I'm starting to worry that they might actually drive right over the top of me, the driver slams on the brakes and stops. Dust kicks up into my face. The Jeep stops so close, I could drop my hand and just about touch the bonnet. For a moment, I have the urge to arrest them both, but I suppose that wouldn't go down too well with the commissioner. Or the military brass.

'Welcome to Wangamba, I'm Sergeant Furey of the Queensland Police,' I say instead, as politely as I can muster. 'As you can see, all the townsfolk have turned out to welcome you into town.'

One of the MPs sniffs.

'So, this is Wrong-jamba, huh? Gee, that's really swell. We made it at last. For a moment I thought we'd driven clean past your state and into the desert.'

The driver's grinning as he looks into the crowd. They're all cheering at the two Americans, while the photographer from *The North Star*'s snapping pictures.

'Wow,' says the passenger. 'We didn't expect a welcoming parade.'

Their faces are caked in dust, and the passenger starts to cough like he's just swallowed the entire Simpson Desert, and then he spits. They both look worn out. From where I'm standing, I glimpse their belts and notice that they're both wearing side-arms.

I put my hands on my hips. 'Well, we're a friendly mob here in Wan-gam-ba,' I reply, making a point of it. 'You'll learn how to say it. One day...'

The driver ignores me. 'I tell you what,' he continues to nobody in particular, 'that trip was a real sonofabitch. Must be the worst road I've ever been on.' He claps eyes on me at last. 'You the sheriff around here, bud?'

'Well, I'm Sergeant Furey of the Queensland Police,' I repeat. 'I'm the senior law officer in the town.'

'Corporal Bishop,' he mutters, 'and my buddy here is Corporal Hoffman. Do I salute you?'

'No, mate, you don't have to do that,' I reply, and then I immediately regret it.

'Great, so we'll just continue on through the town. In that...' The driver's distracted by a pretty girl by the side of the road. 'You'll give us directions?'

I want to warn them against fraternisation, but I suspect they've already been told. I doubt that me saying it again will make the slightest difference. 'My constables will direct you through town to your camp site,' is my only response.

'Thanks, Sarge. You've been a great help,' says Hoffman, but I don't think he means it.

The rest of the convoy is bearing down on us, so I don't want to hold them up too long. They have to set up their base before nightfall.

In front of the town hall, the brass band's warming up again. I hear the strains of 'The Star Spangled Banner'. Or 'The Stars and Stripes Forever'. Or a combination of the two. The din is drowning the MPs out. And just as well, before they cause an international incident.

Bishop puts the Jeep in gear and gets ready to speed off again, but I can't let them drive down the main street on the wrong side of the road. The law is the law.

'Before you head off,' I begin, 'you're going to have to drive on the left side of the road. It's how we drive here.'

'But we drove all the way from Townsville on this side of the road. We didn't have any trouble,' Bishop argues.

For a while, their arrogance floors me.

Hoffman looks amused. 'Buddy,' he says to Bishop, 'I guess we didn't pass any vehicles.' He turns to me, 'Although we did see some cows and a few kangaroos, and they didn't say anything.'

'Consider yourselves lucky,' I reply, trying to look like my word's the law around here, and wishing I'd made them salute me after all. 'You only got away with it because there isn't a lot of traffic on the road. If you want to avoid accidents in the future, Corporal, you'll have to stick to the rules. We drive on the left in this country.'

Bishop continues, 'Well, we're Americans, and we drive on the right. That's our law. We don't have to listen to some hayseed telling us what to do. You should be lucky we're here to help you guys at all.'

I can't believe what I'm hearing. 'In this country, we all drive on the left-hand side of the road. No exceptions,' I emphasise, 'not even for Americans.'

I haven't shifted an inch from where I started.

Bishop revs the engine once, but I don't move. He then starts swearing and revving the Jeep continuously. I can hear him cursing above the noise of the engine. He edges closer until the bumper bar touches my knee.

Forget it, Yank, I'm still not budging.

The rest of the convoy has just about caught up and is now approaching us. The first vehicle to pull up behind the Jeep is a staff officer's car. It's so thick with grey silt that its colour's a mystery. The rest of the convoy lumbers to a stop behind that. I estimate there must be thirty to forty troop carriers lined up, loaded to the gunnels with thirsty men and all of their equipment. Apparently, this is just the advance party. The rest of it—the tractors, graders, building supplies and the remainder—will be coming by Queensland Rail from Townsville.

Both of the MPs leap out of the Jeep like cattle dogs. Bishop stands to attention next to the Jeep and Hoffman rushes over to open the rear door of the staff car, his right arm stiff in salute. The bloke inside must be pretty important, I'm thinking. I notice the driver before I notice him. And who wouldn't? She's nothing like my Gracie. She's a bit of a sort. She's wearing a cap, but even through the dirty windscreen I can see her permed blonde hair poking out underneath it, and her rouged lips. I'm thinking she looks a lot like Carole Landis.

An airforce officer steps out. He's immaculate: clean-cut, sweatless and untouched by the trip. His tunic fits like a glove. It looks tailor-made. In fact, from cap to boot, he looks tailor-made. He takes off his sunglasses and salutes Hoffman back. It's like he just stepped off a movie set. You know, like one of those war movies they make these days in Hollywood. He's the hero, and the hero never dies.

The officer rolls over to me. He's covered in as many medals as Douglas MacArthur and walks like he has six shooters on each hip. I hide a chuckle in the palm of my hand, and wonder whether to greet him or line up for a shoot-out. Bishop follows him like a pup.

'Is there a problem here, Corporal Bishop?' he drawls.

Sounds to me like he's from one of the confederate states. I remember the way they draw out their vowels, like what they have to say is somehow more important than anything anyone else has to say. I haven't heard that accent in twenty-four years but I haven't forgotten it, and it's just as hard to understand now as it was then. Yep, I met a few of them on leave, back in 1918. Not bad blokes, really. To be honest, they were a bit better behaved than us Diggers. I reckon we had tickets on ourselves back then, because we were a volunteer army and they weren't.

I'm guessing the officer could be above a captain, although I don't know their rank system very well. He seems pretty high up, by the way the MPs are fawning over him.

'The police sergeant, here,' Bishop says as he points at me like I'm a naughty child, 'says we're driving on the wrong side of the road, Colonel. He says from now on we have to drive on the right side of the road, and that the right side is the left side, sir.'

'That's how we do things here, Colonel,' I interrupt. 'I'm Sergeant Jack Furey of the Queensland Police. We drive on the left in Australia. It's plain and simple.'

Bishop grows crimson with rage, but I don't give a toss about that.

Let him blow his fufu valve.

The officer looks me up and down, sizing me up. He's an imposing man, standing about six foot with broad shoulders. I stand five-eight. He takes particular interest in my medals.

'Colonel Reynolds, United States Air Force,' he belts out. 'It's an honour, Sergeant Furey.'

He shakes my hand vigorously as Bishop stares at him, confused.

'An honour, Colonel?' I question.

'That's a Military Medal you have there.'

'Yes, Colonel. I got it at the Battle of Hamel in 1918.'

He looks pleased, and that just makes Bishop look displeased.

'I was there too,' he says. 'A hell of a battle. Glad we got it over quickly.'

'Yep,' I reply, remembering the sound of exploding shells and the crack of the trees falling all around us. 'Lost a few mates that day.'

'Me too, Sergeant. Me too.' Colonel Reynolds looks sad, and that just makes Bishop look dismal. 'So we're partners, huh? You must come over for a drink when we get the base set up, Sergeant.'

'Yes,' I reply. I can't tell if he means it. 'I'll look forward to it. You better continue on. I think the band's played "Stars and Stripes" for the third time. They'll probably run out of puff soon.'

'Is that what that was?' He looks around. 'And what's with the welcoming committee? We're here on military business. This was supposed to be on the quiet.'

I'm already shaking my head. 'Yes, sir, I know. I had orders to tell the mayor and, well…' I can see he understands. 'Well, he's that sort of bloke. Perhaps, you'd better take it up with him.'

Reynolds takes his cap off, scratches his head and puts his cap and his sunglasses back on. 'I bet the sonofabitch hasn't done a day's service. There won't be any parties and celebrations today, or any other day. We have a war to win. Thank you, Sergeant.'

He throws me a salute and I return it. I haven't done that for a while.

'And about the left side of the road?' I ask quietly.

'Of course, Sergeant. We're here to work together. We're allies and we're mates, as you Aussies say.'

'Thank you, Colonel. And welcome again to Wangamba.'

Reynolds spins on his heel and walks back to the staff car. He calls Bishop aside. I pretend not to hear him tell Bishop that he doesn't want to see him or Hoffman obstructing the local police again. 'If Sergeant Furey gives you or your MPs a damn direction, you darn well obey it!' he barks. 'Understood?'

'Yes, Colonel, sir!' Bishop stammers.

'And make sure you take a good look at the Sergeant. That's what a genuine war hero looks like. Something I suspect you'll never be.'

'Yes, sir, Colonel!'

'Now open my goddamned door. We've wasted enough time.'

I reckon I'll be able to work with him just fine. He's direct. I like the way he does things. There are no flies on the colonel. I look around, but I can't spot Gracie or our son, so I don't think they'll get to see the colonel today. She'd have been chuffed to have seen him talking to me.

The convoy heads off as 'The Star Spangled Banner' starts up. Above the roar of the vehicles, the crowd's cheering so loud that you'd be excused for thinking that the local team's playing in the Grand Final. I watch them rumble down the street, drowning out the tortured tones of the brass band. As the colonel's car climbs the hill, slowing down a little to pass the mayor and councillors, I have a chuckle to myself. Even from down here, I can see their mouths drop open and their stunned resignation as the car just keeps going.

I wonder what Mayor Jessop will make of that.

CHAPTER THREE

I heard that the Americans built their base in eight days—in just eight days—so I reckon Colonel Reynolds must be cracking the whip. Once the machinery arrived on the train, it was on for young and old, and our civil engineers pulled out all the stops to finish the airfield in a matter of weeks after that.

After it was done, the colonel rang me up and asked me over to have a drink at their canteen and a chin-wag. I'm up for it. I need to get away from the trucks and the dust and the silliness. I've been working more hours than I should, and I haven't seen much of Gracie or the boy lately. A boy needs his father, but I've been running around like a blue-arsed fly, trying to make sure that things run smoothly in Wangamba for everyone: the locals as well as the Americans.

I'm only going to have one or two beers. No harm in that, is there?

So I'm off to visit the Americans.

I arrive at the airfield, not really knowing what to expect. A couple of Douglas DC-3s flew in here yesterday and Snowy McIntyre, silly old bugger, thought they were Japs. He jumped the gun and rang the siren and it was all on for young and old. What idiot thought he'd be a good choice for air warden?

The planes passed low over the town, and I could see a star insignia on the fuselage, so I assumed they were American. The boys and I were eventually able to reassure most of the locals that they weren't Japs after all, though some of those who went in the shelter didn't want to come out.

If you see a big, bloody red dot on a plane, then you worry, but as for the rest of them… Well, they're friends, I reckon.

Anyway, I had a quiet word to Snowy after the incident and told him to pull his head in. Obviously he hasn't got his copy of the aircraft recognition book from the government yet. I'll make sure he does, otherwise we'll have pandemonium every time an aircraft flies in.

The DC-3s are parked on the airstrip to my right, and I've got to say that they're impressive looking aircraft up close. I'd love to have taken Gracie and the boy for a trip in one of them, back when they were flying between Australia and the continent, before the war. I suppose that'll have to wait for better days.

There are trucks dotted all around the airstrip and a couple of men up in the control tower, watching the sky with their binoculars. The base looks pretty lively: men and vehicles constantly on the move.

Gracie's disappointed that she hasn't clapped eyes on the colonel yet, and she doesn't believe me when I say that he looks like Gary Cooper. To be honest, no one's seen him around town since the parade, and now I know why. Most of the igloo huts are built now, so there are only a few of the pitched tents here and there to house the infantrymen. I bet they're happy about that. This spot's always been thick with snakes. I'd bet a pound to a penny that they'd have met a few of them by now, which probably accounts for the swiftness of the build.

I heard that the colonel's commandeered the top rooms at the Royal Hotel for himself and his subordinate officers, and that his driver is on the same floor, but I can't confirm it. I guess she needs to be close by in case he wants to go somewhere fast. The accommodation arrangements haven't gone unnoticed. Got some tongues wagging, I'll tell you.

I take some time to survey the landscape. The camp has everything that opens and shuts: mess hall, first aid, canteen, maintenance sheds and toilet blocks. None of those outdoor dunnies out here, like the ones we have to put up with. Yep, they've got all the modern conveniences. You've got to hand it to Colonel Reynolds, he really knows how to get things done.

I look around for any other luncheon guests, but it's only me so far, which is good.

The colonel meets me at the front of the administration office. I notice that Carole Landis isn't with him. I'd ask where she is, but he might think that was a bit rude. He's decked out immaculately. As usual.

'Sergeant Furey.' He smiles widely as he shakes my hand. 'Glad you could make it at such short notice.' He seems pretty happy to see me.

'Thanks for the invite. Call me Jack. I'm not much for formalities,' I explain, although I get the feeling that he probably is.

'And neither am I.' He laughs, but he never requests that I call him Frank. His eyes are focused on something way over my head, in the distance. 'I couldn't mention it when I called, but today's a red-letter day,' he continues. 'The first of the aircraft will be flying in from Brisbane. They should be here within the hour.' He checks his watch.

'Not expecting anyone else, Colonel?' I comment. 'I thought Mayor Jessop…'

He's shaking his head. 'Naturally, I will, in due course.' He slaps my shoulder lightly and leads me away. 'We'll need to iron a few things out, build a good relationship first, you and I. No reason to bring in the politicians yet, is there? You have an important job to do, and I want to make sure our boys know who you are, and that they respect your position. I don't want them running amok like they own the place. I know how country folk can be.'

I say, 'Well, boys will be boys, but I'm optimistic…'

The Yanks haven't had any leave yet so it's been pretty quiet in town so far, but I reckon they're going to want to tear one on, when they do. Once they hit town, I reckon the local businesses will be doing all right out of this friendly invasion, especially the five pubs, four cafes and the cinema. Although I don't know if the Yanks will fare quite as well with the beer, the plain food and the three-year-old movie pictures.

He's distracted again.

'…that everyone will behave themselves, Colonel.'

There are three necessities, in my experience, for keeping a serviceman happy: keep them fed, keep them watered and keep them entertained. Same as in Roman times.

'We're both men of the world. All I can say, as far as the horizontal refreshment goes, is that the boys better keep their urges under control when it comes to our girls, you know what I mean. I don't want Wangamba to get a reputation for being free-and-easy. Brisbane can have that one.'

'We both run a tight ship. We're on the same page,' he replies, 'and that's a good thing.'

I suppose I have to be realistic. Like any other place, we have our fair share of loose women. Town bikes, we call them here, and we all know who they are. I blame their poor upbringing and bad parents for that. The thing is, there aren't enough town bikes to keep all of the Yanks happy—as far as I know—and I certainly don't want any of our decent girls chasing after them.

'This is a respectable, church-going town, not Sodom and Gomorrah,' I continue.

'Yes, yes, of course,' he replies.

I'm thinking that the boys had better get used to the deep affections of Mrs Palmer and Her Five Daughters. I'm not stupid, but I expect that the servicemen will behave better here than the Diggers did during the Great War, tossing prozzies off balconies, and burning down the Cairo brothel district, over a syphilitic whore.

I don't care who you are or where you came from, I'll be still planting my number ten boot right up your arse and giving you a whack on your thick noggin with my night stick. So don't step out of line.

His eyes return to me. 'Feel like something to eat, Jack? We have time before the aircraft land.'

We head towards the mess hall. I can smell steaks cooking and my stomach gurgles. 'Right now, I could eat a horse and chase the rider.'

He smiles again, although I'm not certain he really understands what I'm on about.

There are already several officers in the mess hall. They're standing at the bar, and opposite them are four black stewards, wiping counters and filling orders. They all stand to attention when Colonel Reynolds and I enter.

He puffs himself up another few inches. 'Gentlemen, at ease,' he announces. 'Allow me to introduce you to my special guest, Sergeant Jack Furey. Sergeant Furey is an officer of the Queensland Police Force. He is responsible for keeping law and order in Wangamba, and he's also a war hero, so I suggest you try to stay on his good side.'

The men titter, and my collar starts to feel tight.

'It happens that he and I served together in France during World War One, although we were both ignorant of the fact until the other day. I say he's a war hero, since Sergeant Furey is the recipient of the Military Medal, one of the highest bravery awards in the British Army. Gentlemen, I urge you to obey his lawful orders, and not to underestimate his resolve. I know from personal experience that Australians are tough fighters. We should all be glad they're on our side. Please welcome him to the mess.'

The officers' claps sound like rain on an iron roof. I feel embarrassed.

'Carry on, men,' he continues.

I'm glad he doesn't expect a speech.

He turns to me again. 'What will you have to drink, Jack? Bourbon, beer or whisky? It's American beer, I'm afraid. We haven't quite adapted to your beer, yet.'

There's plenty of grog and food out here. 'A beer would be nice,' I reply.

I look at the officers' fresh faces and realise how young they are, and that they're going to be fighting—and some of them are going to be dying—soon. So let them have their enjoyment, I say.

'I feel a bit out of place here, Colonel, a bit of a blow-in. I've never been in an officers' mess. I was only ever a sergeant…'

Reynolds smiles. His arm's on my shoulder. 'You're my guest and that's the highest rank on my base.' He calls over a steward who is gathering empty glasses from the officers. 'You're always welcome here, Jack.'

For a moment I feel like I'm in one of those posh hotels in Sydney or Melbourne: the places where silvertails stay. I'd like to be able bring Gracie here for a slap-up meal. She'd be thrilled to have a reason to dress up to the nines.

'Hey, boy,' he calls out, 'a whisky! Make it the way I like it, and bring over a Budweiser for the sergeant. And for Chrissakes, this time, make sure the beer is cold.'

'Yessir,' the steward replies softly, scurrying away to the bar.

'The last beer he served was warm as piss,' he observes. He doesn't seem to notice that the boy never looked at him. 'You undoubtedly noticed the Negro labour squad rolled in the other day, to speed up the construction,' he goes on.

'I saw them come on a mob of trucks late in the afternoon. They drove down the main street heading out to the airfield. Funny, there was no mayoral welcome and no brass band for them,' I reply, and the colonel's eyes cloud over, even as I speak. 'Some of the locals in the street stared at them, but that was about it. Those boys looked pretty miserable. They probably hadn't even heard of Australia before they got here.'

'And why should they? They have enough trouble beating the three Rs into them back home, without needing to teach them geography besides.'

I heard tell that the blacks have been segregated into their own camp, but I don't tell Colonel Reynolds that. Whites and blacks don't mix much in civilian life back in America, so I guess that they've just carried that over into the military. It's not that different here, I suppose, although when I served with Aboriginal servicemen in the Great War, they were billeted just the same as we were. I look at the stewards again, and they don't seem bothered by the difference in their station, so why should I be? At least they're getting regular meals, good pay and a warm bed, and that's probably a damn sight better than the way they're treated back home.

Maybe it won't be too bad for them out here.

'You know,' he starts up again, 'blacks will never be more than stewards and labourers in this war and, in my experience, that's all they're capable of being.' He looks smug. 'If you give them guns, chances are, they'll turn them on us. Or at best, they'll shoot themselves by mistake. I'm damn proud that my family has owned the biggest plantation in Virginia for hundreds of years, and why shouldn't I be? We knew how to treat our niggers. Everyone had their place until the damned Yankees destroyed our way of life. Those sons of bitches really ruined the South.'

I'm wondering if I should take as an example of their way of life, all of those white blokes running around dressed in bed sheets with pointy caps over their heads, holding torches and burning crosses. I don't understand any of it. It all sounds nasty and childish to me. I stopped pulling the sheets over my head and frightening people when I was a little tacker, and I never once thought about hanging anybody from a tree, black or white.

He eyes me off. 'What do you think, Jack, of niggers in the military?'

'I'm surprised that you're fighting for the Yanks,' I chuckle, avoiding his question, and hoping he doesn't notice.

'I'm fighting for my country, which just happens to be the United States of America. I'd prefer it was the Confederacy, but the reality is that those yellow-bellied Yankees wouldn't be able win an arm-wrestling competition without us doing all their heavy fighting.'

My beer arrives and I take a long sip. 'Not bad. Better than ours. Ours tastes like cat piss.'

The ice in his whisky clinks. 'So, what do you think of niggers in the military?' he repeats.

'Don't know much about your history, I'm afraid,' I lie. 'There were some Aborigines in our battalion in France and they fought bloody hard. At first I thought they might run away but they didn't. I don't mind them in the military, although I wouldn't want one of them marrying a daughter of mine, if you know what I mean.'

'Well, you must have yours better trained,' he laughs before sipping his whisky. 'They have to know their place in the natural order of the races. Gorillas don't mix with wart hogs, do they?'

Just then, the chief steward announces that lunch is ready.

'Time to eat, Jack,' Reynolds proclaims, slapping me on the back.

We sit down at the head table. After a blessing, the food comes out on large trays. I can't believe the amount of food they've dished up. You could have fed the whole town. I don't complain when they plonk the biggest steak I've ever seen onto my plate, along with a mountain of cooked vegetables, some of which I don't recognise.

'I didn't ask how you wanted your steak done, Jack,' he says, cutting into his.

I slice into it and notice it's medium. I'd have preferred well-done, but I'm not bloody complaining. 'It's fine, as long as I can't see the whip marks.'

Reynolds laughs.

I point my knife at a heap of shiny orange discs too big to be carrots. 'I'm not sure what these are,' I say quietly.

Reynolds looks at my plate. 'That vegetable is candied yam. It's popular in the South. We wanted to bring a bit of the South here, so we wouldn't get too homesick. Just like me, many of my men are from there.'

'I'll give them a go,' I reply as I tuck in. They're sweet and heavy with cinnamon, like someone's mixed dessert up with my main meal. I'm thinking that they would probably be all right if my steak wasn't bleeding into them. 'Not bad. I'll have to tell the missus about it.'

We eat for a bit before I speak again. 'So, you were in the army during World War One. Is that why you changed over to the air force?' I ask.

'That war was hell on earth. I never wanted to see a war like that again,' he replies. There's sadness in his delivery.

'It was a bastard, all right. How I got through it still amazes me. Many of my mates didn't. Poor buggers. Still have bloody nightmares about being there,' I admit.

He raises his glass. 'To mates!'

'To mateship,' I respond.

We polish off our glasses, and a steward quickly replenishes them.

'I come from a military family and we have proudly served our country since the War of Independence,' Reynolds continues. 'But after the war, I thought I could best serve my country by being part of the air force. Here's something for nothing: the sky is the future of war. A strong air force could save thousands of lives.'

'I tell you what, it seems pretty glamorous from down here. There's a look to the planes and those uniforms. I reckon I'd give it a go if were a bit younger,' I reply. 'Dropping bombs on those bastards has got to be better than having to kill them up close; you get to stay clean, eat a decent meal and sleep in a bed at the end of the day.'

'When we get settled in, Jack, I'll take you up for a joy flight in one of our B-25s. How'd that be?'

'That would be great. I'll look forward to it.' I take another bite and push some of the yams under a pile of limp boiled greens. 'B-25? Which bomber is that?'

'The Mitchell. The ones they used in the Doolittle Raid. The ones that dropped bombs on those yellow bastards in Tokyo.'

I know he's right about the air force being the way of the future. 'I reckon that this war and every one after it will be decided by who has the greatest air power.'

He lifts up his empty glass and jiggles it. 'I never again want to see trench warfare and good men drowning in mud, just to gain a few yards of ground.'

'I hope this war is over soon, Colonel,' I reply before finishing off my steak. 'Makes me mad to read the paper nowadays, what with news of the Japanese bombing Batavia and Burma, and wondering if we'll be next. Every so often I wish I was back in the army, just so if they do get here, I could run a few of them through with a bayonet. You just never know what they're thinking behind those eyes. No emotion, you see. Everyone thinks the Germans are cruel, but I reckon the Japs are worse than the Huns.'

'Well, you won't have to worry about them arriving on Australian shores, at least, not anymore. We've got it all in hand.'

As I accept another beer, he takes a sip out of his third whisky soda, but who's counting. I'm as full as a house and ease my belt a notch, when he tells me that there's dessert. Bloody hell! I nearly say it aloud, when I spot the stewards bringing it out. Apple pie and ice cream. And not a small dish of it, either.

'Now, I don't want you getting the wrong idea,' he chuckles, as the steward puts the bowl down in front of me. 'We don't get this every day out here.'

Thank God, I've found enough space for it. I start on it slowly, pacing myself for the finish. By the end of the meal I'm chockers, as full as a poisoned pup. I feel like crawling under a tree and having a camp.

I suspect that Reynolds feels it too. He tilts his chair back a bit. 'And Corporals Bishop and Hoffman have been behaving themselves?'

'No complaints so far,' I reply. 'All you see these days are trucks going everywhere around town, from early morning until dark. My wife Gracie was complaining about how the trucks were making the house dusty, until the council finally pulled their lazy fingers out and started watering down the roads. At least the dust's settled for a while.'

He pulls out a wooden pick and prods at his tooth, but doesn't respond.

'Sometimes the trucks speed like billy-o, but at least they're travelling on the left. Along with my blokes, the military police do a pretty good job directing the traffic. We keep them in close check. I've heard stories of a few of the Townsville locals getting run over. So far I've heard that there have been three fatalities. Bloody awful.'

'Hmm,' he says carelessly. 'Casualties of war.'

I feel my eyebrows rise. 'Something else has been worrying me a bit lately. See, the thing is, we have enough of our own blackfellas around here to sort out and I don't know how it's going to go having more of them.'

Most of the time ours are quiet, but they can get drunk and disorderly sometimes, and they can have the odd fight. Some of them are decent, hospitable blokes, but they're not settled, like us. I can't understand why they want to live the way they do.

'You concerned that you'll have problems with the Negroes?' he asks.

'I don't know too much about their nature. Everyone knows that Aborigines can't handle the grog, but the pubs sell it to them anyway on the sly, just so they can make a few more quid. I don't want that happening with yours, too.'

God help those publicans, if I catch up with them.

I have a strong suspicion that Harry Barlow at *The Sovereign* is one of them, but I can't quite pin it on him yet. He'll be well and truly in the gun when I nab him.

I tell Reynolds that what I'm most worried about is that some of the black Americans might want to get in amongst our women. I say, 'I heard that they're uncontrollable in that way. I know they like to dance, laugh, sing and carry on, and I don't think their music helps them much. I don't think that way of living is very moral and it won't be happening on my watch.'

'Well,' he replies, 'the MPs know that they'll have to keep them in check. All that wild jazz music would send anyone a little funny in the head. I don't want to go into it too much, but their animal urges can get the better of them. I don't want you to worry about it, Jack. We've got them in hand, too.'

I'm still pushing away my dessert bowl when an officer walks briskly into the mess and whispers into the colonel's ear.

'They're approaching,' Reynolds mutters, wipes his lips with the napkin and stands up.

The officers watch like eagles as he pulls back his chair and jumps to his feet.

'Gentlemen,' he declares, 'our boys are on the approach. We have work to do.' He taps me on the arm. 'You too, Jack. The bombers are coming.'

I'm on my feet and raring to go. I'm as keen as mustard to see them.

I follow the colonel out of the mess, only barely aware that it's emptied behind us and that everyone's assembling at the base of the control tower. Among the steely clouds, I can just make out a group of planes coming in from the west. They hadn't followed the coast. I can't yet work out what they are or how many, but they seem to stretch out a long way. I can faintly hear the hum of their motors.

'The inland route's the quickest. No surprise there,' I mumble.

A junior officer hands Reynolds a pair of binoculars. 'Great!' He counts off twelve.

'They're going into their final approach, sir,' the officer comments.

'It's good to see them again,' he says jubilantly.

The planes tip their wings and wheel towards the airfield one by one, and it reminds me of a Busby Berkeley dance routine.

'Here, take a look, Jack.' Reynolds hands me his binoculars.

As the clouds part, the sun makes the newly dried concrete sparkle. I adjust my focus. 'They're huge!' I can't believe how big the buggers are. Then again, the only aircraft we see around here are Flying Doctors' planes and the occasional Tiger Moth. The bombers are streamlined and sleek with their combat colours: a big white star stamped on the fuselage. I spot the machine guns sticking out of them. It's overwhelming and I feel myself oddly tearing up. I hand the binoculars back to him.

One after another they touch down on the tarmac, as lightly as ducks on a pond. Whenever the tyres of the Mitchell aircraft screech, the men whistle and cheer.

'See,' says Reynolds, his eyes gleaming, 'I told you that the Japs don't stand a chance now that we're here.'

One by one, eleven planes land without incident and taxi to their allocated spots, as men peel off from the crowd to assist the ground crews and to welcome them, until there's just one left to land. He's lagging behind. I'm no expert on planes, but he looks to be in a bit of trouble. I strain my eyes.

Someone in the control tower hangs half his body out of a window and yells, 'Colonel, sir, there's smoke coming from the starboard engine!'

'I see it…I see it…Goddamn it,' he mutters. He shouts back, 'Bring this baby home. I'm counting on you, son.'

The pilot makes an approach but then suddenly pulls the plane up again. I glimpse its nose art as it flies past me. It has *Missouri Mama* painted on the side in leery colours. I can see one of the pilot's heads.

The Mitchell rounds the airfield again.

'Ease her down!' Reynolds bellows. 'Come on, son, you can do it!' His eyes follow the plane as it circles overhead.

I hear someone cry, 'The engine's on fire!'

Reynolds shudders. 'So, what are you waiting for? Get the crash truck and the ambulance on the runway now!'

A few of the men scramble off and, soon after, both vehicles speed onto the tarmac.

'She's coming in again. If you're a praying man, Jack, this would be the time…'

The Mitchell makes another approach and it's trailing thick, black smoke. The fire in the engine has really taken hold. I can see flames running along the wing. My heart is in my mouth.

Dear Lord in heaven…

Reynolds says, 'The approach is better. They're good pilots, Gentry and Morrissey. If they can't bring her in on one engine, no one can.'

The plane comes down so slowly that I find myself looking for the string tying it to the sky. The right propeller isn't spinning: the engine's swallowed up by flames. It only has a few hundred feet to go, but the fire's creeping towards the fuselage. The Mitchell shakes a little, the burning wing has dipped and the plane's flying on an angle.

'It's going to be a rough landing,' someone says.

The Mitchell doesn't touch down, it skips. The fire doesn't look quite as ferocious as it eases down the tarmac. I hold my breath as it takes the entire length of the airstrip to slow down, hoping it won't end up in the bush.

The Mitchell eventually comes to a dead stop at the far end of the tarmac and the crash truck sprays a stream of foam over the wing and the engine. Reynolds sprints towards the plane like a young man, ignoring shouted warnings that the plane might explode, and

I find myself, and half of the men around me, doing the same. Even before the fire's out, men are climbing up the other side to open the canopy and help the crew out. By the time the rest of us get close, almost half of the plane's covered in foam and Reynolds is smiling and slapping backs. The pilot is crouched down, hugging his knees, surrounded by his crew. I can see the strain on their baby faces.

I'm amazed none of them is injured.

Reynolds sucks his cheeks. 'One out of action, and we haven't even started fighting the Japs yet,' he says to me.

'There are always going to be accidents, Colonel,' I reply.

Bloody hell, I didn't realise how bloody dangerous it could be. I take my hat off to them.

'As long as we don't have too many. So, how do you feel about going up in one now?' he asks.

'I'll let you know,' I reply hesitantly.

CHAPTER FOUR

'Somebody's asking to speak to you, Sergeant.'

Higgins's uniform is open at the collar. It makes us look slovenly.

'Asking to see me?' I reply. 'Did you get a name?'

'I asked, but she wouldn't say. She was a bit stirred up, by the look of her.'

'Right.' I push away from my desk and stand up, wondering which do-gooder has decided that today is a good day to inform on what the neighbours got up to over the weekend. 'And for goodness sake, Constable, do up your top button.'

He grimaces. 'But it's too tight, Sergeant. It makes me feel like I'm choking.'

'I'm not your mother, Constable Higgins. I don't care if it chokes you until you're blue in the face. Button up. It's the uniform.'

I leave Higgins struggling with his button and go out to the counter. A woman I don't recognise stands opposite me. She sports a platinum bob, cupid's bow lips and pencilled eyebrows. It's as if the twenties never left us.

'You in charge here?' Her voice grates. She fiddles with her bag and pulls out a cigarette case.

'Sergeant Furey. And you can't smoke in here.'

'Why ever not?' she asks. 'It calms my nerves. And believe me, they need calming.'

'Regardless. No smoking, Mrs…'

She pouts and slips the case back into her bag. 'Mrs Singleton.'

'I don't know you. You new to town, Mrs Singleton?' I look at her from top to toe. *Jean Harlow.* Cloche hat, gloves and a cotton dress: a bit old-fashioned, but she's dressed soberly enough. 'So, what can I do you for?'

'I just moved into a house on King Street last week. Me and my two girls. The climate here agrees with me, you see. Not as humid out here as on the coast.' She waves her hand about, like she's swatting flies. 'I'm a widow, you see, Mr Furey, minding my own business. This morning, I come out to sweep my front step and I find this.'

I'm about to correct her when she heaves a cardboard box onto the counter, and places her handbag next to it.

'Left at my door.'

The box has nothing on it. I don't quite know what I'm about to see. I tilt the box, peer inside and take a step backwards. 'Is it…a baby?'

'Looks like a baby to me,' she says dryly.

I take another look. Its eyes are shut. It's barely weeks old, possibly only days. 'But not yours?'

She rolls her eyes, and for once I have to agree that I would have done the same in reply to my question. As well preserved as she is, she's clearly beyond childbearing. I take another look at the contents of the box. The baby's swaddled in a grubby towel. It's barely breathing, but it seems to be alive.

I ask, 'You don't happen to know whose it is?'

She's brittle. 'Well, I wouldn't have brought it here if I did. All I know is, the box was on my doorstep when I got up this morning. I've done my bit and brought it in and, as I see it, now it's your responsibility.'

I bellow for a constable, and Mahoney appears beside me at the desk. I point at the box. He gasps at the sight of the baby. 'Take the baby quick, down to the hospital as fast as you can, Constable.

Apparently, it's a foundling.'

Mahoney lifts the box gingerly.

'Quick, man. It's a baby, not a bomb! God only knows how long it's been since it was last fed and watered,' I growl. 'It's an emergency. Push yourself ahead of anyone else, even if you have to pull rank, and be sure to tell the nurse that.'

He places the box under his arm and scurries out of the station and down the street, as Mrs Singleton picks up her bag and turns to leave.

'Just a minute, Mrs Singleton, I'd like to take your statement before you go. For the record, you understand.' I try to sound sympathetic.

'I'm a busy woman, Mr Furey, I really don't have time…'

I drop the sympathy. 'It's Sergeant Furey, Mrs Singleton, and I really must insist… Something you tell us might help us find the baby's mother.'

She taps the counter with her lacquered nails. 'I'm no mind reader, Sergeant, but I'd say she doesn't want to be found.'

'Well, regardless, we'll have to try to find her. The interview won't take long, and then you can be on your way.'

She scowls. 'I don't think you understand. I don't want to get involved,' she mutters.

Something's unsettled her. I start to wonder if the baby might not belong to one of her daughters.

'Too late,' I tell her, 'you already are.'

CHAPTER FIVE

Gracie's already heard about the foundling before I even have the chance to get home. Her eyes are bright, and I know something's playing on her mind, but she doesn't say much beyond, 'I pity the poor woman who gave up her child. Who on God's sweet earth would do such a thing?'

I tell her that the baby is a little girl, she wasn't set adrift, and she isn't about to lead anyone into the promised land, that's for certain.

Gracie sniffs and sets the table. She doles out a stew made of scrag-end and potatoes, and still makes it taste like a plateful of heaven.

Once we've finished our dinner and our boy's left the table, she asks me what's to become of the baby.

'Well, that depends on a few things,' I reply. 'Firstly, the baby's had a bit of a rough ride. She's still in hospital, and they don't know if she'll survive. Even if she does, they say that she may be retarded.'

I don't tell her that the doctor thinks the mother may have tried to strangle her baby with the umbilical cord, before apparently leaving her in a box on a stranger's doorstep overnight to die.

I continue, 'If she does survive, then we'll be searching for her mother.'

I don't tell her that we'll be searching for her mother in order to have her committed as a lunatic.

Gracie sighs. 'I believe she's a sign to all that we need to keep our hearts open, even in this troubled time, and that we must be slow to judge the actions of others.'

She gathers up the plates and I follow her into the kitchen, where the boy's tucked up on a chair with his knees under his chin, reading a book. Just like his dad. As a kid, I could never find enough books to read. When school failed me, I began reading everything and anything, and I guess I never stopped.

She turns to him. 'Do be a dear, and go read your book in the other room, Mikey. Your father and I have things to discuss.'

Mikey throws me a look which suggests to me that he thinks the discussion will centre around him. He thinks he's done something wrong. I shake my head, but it only makes it worse.

'Don't worry, lad, it's not about you.'

'Then why can't I stay and listen?' he asks me.

'Adult talk, Mikey. Not fit for young ears.'

He groans and leaves the room. For good measure, I shut the door behind him.

I pick up the tea towel and settle next to the sink. 'I need your help with this one, Gracie. I suspect that the mother of the child isn't married and she may be a local woman. We asked the doctor and the nurses, but no one knows of anyone due to have a baby about now, and no woman has come in for any treatment since. It makes me think that she might be young.'

'Perhaps she isn't a local after all,' says Gracie.

'Wangamba's too far from everywhere else and it's too small for a woman to come to on purpose, just to give birth. If she wanted to go some place where her condition wouldn't be discovered, she'd be far better off in a big town. That's why I think she's a local lass and that's why I think she's young.'

'You may be right. Possibly the poor girl didn't even realise what was happening to her.' She looks away, plugs the sink and runs the tap. 'So what do you want me to do?'

'I need you to remember. I want you to think back over the last few months. Perhaps you might have seen one of our young ladies in the family way and trying to hide it? Perhaps you might have noticed her in church, or at the shops?'

'I don't know… I'll have to mull it over,' she begins. 'I'll keep my eyes peeled.'

'She's only recently had the baby, so you may hear of someone's daughter doing poorly.'

'Well, if I do, I'll let you know.' She hands me a wet plate. 'If the baby does survive, and if you don't find the mother, or if she doesn't want the baby… Well, do you think we might be able to raise her?'

'That's an awful lot of ifs, Gracie, and don't forget she could well be a handful. I don't think it's something we should do.'

'Hmm.'

I can tell the thought hasn't left her mind. 'Let's not discuss it tonight. There'll be plenty of time for us to talk it over,' I say, although my mind is dead set against it. 'In the meantime…'

'Don't worry,' she replies, 'If I hear something…'

She looks away and never finishes the sentence.

CHAPTER SIX

The Royal Australian Air Force has just finished building its airfield, out near the river. It's a bit late, but at least it's done. I went out there the other day to have a look, but they wouldn't even let me through the main gate. That's a nice bloody welcome, isn't it? I guess they can't be too careful. I suppose if you squint really hard on a dark, rainy night, I could just about pass for a Jap spy.

I heard that they're flying Beaufort bombers out of there, flying them up to New Guinea and dropping bombs on the Japs. I also heard that the Australian Army is building a camp not far away from the airfield for soldiers coming back here from the Middle East. Sort of a rest stop before they get jungle training up north, after which they'll be sent to New Guinea. Good thing too, because that campaign's balanced on a knife's edge.

The thing about war you can bank on, is that it's good for business. Wangamba's booming again. Mayor Jessop announced that one of the department stores that has stood empty for years, is about to be turned into a dance hall. I don't know what to make of it. The mayor gets behind just about anything. Me, I hear about these things and I feel a bit sick in the stomach. You know, I'm always anticipating trouble. But that's just me, I suppose.

Sugar's the latest rationing conscript along with tea, and Gracie's worried that her stockpile won't last out the war. I tell her that we'll be right, although I'm thinking of taking up horticulture and bee-keeping as a hobby, just in case. She reckons that by the time I get to constructing a hive, the war'll be over. She's probably right. I might just start building it as a lucky charm.

I haven't seen Reynolds much since the base has got going. I wonder if Carole Landis minds that he's staying out at the base more, rather than in his hotel room. He hasn't made good on his promise to take me up in one of his planes yet, but I imagine that's only because he's a busy man. These days, so am I.

I heard through channels that one of the bombers got shot down over New Guinea, and immediately thought of the *Missouri Mama*. Of course it was a different bomber and a different crew, but even though it wasn't Gentry and Morrissey this time, I bet the six boys who died were just as young and just as eager, and they also had mothers and fathers back home to mourn each one of them. I hope it was quick and they didn't know about it.

You won't see anything about it in *The North Star*; everything is heavily censored now.

Yep, war makes you a busy man. It also makes you a sad man, if you let it.

I finish my tea and head out of the station for a walk around. My constables are doing the same. We try not to drive around too much because of the rationing, but I'm determined to let everyone know we're still the law and we're still here. I've asked for more constables, but the bosses tell me that they'll be impossible to get, now that a lot of blokes have joined up.

I tell my boys that except for us, there'll be outright anarchy.

A council truck is spraying water on the street to settle the dust, after the shopkeepers complained about it ruining their merchandise. Ma Guthrie at the grocery store is frantically cleaning her windows again and she perks up when I wave hello.

I see the same old faces in the same old streets. I head past the cinema and chase away a mob of goats eating a movie poster. Bloody things! They were brought in during the gold rush, except that when the miners left, the goats stayed and they're a bloody nuisance. The Yanks have run over a few. Shame that there aren't more people hungry for goat meat these days, like there were during the Depression. Perhaps old Jessop could make himself useful and think of a way to get rid of them.

I get to the top of the street and notice four women getting out of a flash-looking car. It's a Buick, black, just like the one the owner of Wicklow Downs Station drives. After a second glance, I know it's not the same car. It seems that the ladies are headed for Mayberry's Dress Shoppe. Whoever they are, they must have a few quid on them: that Buick's got to cost hundreds of pounds.

I stroll up to take a closer look. The girls are in their twenties, dolled up to the nines. They're all wearing hats and gloves, stockings and high heels, like they're about to go to some posh restaurant, or to the races.

I'm thinking Gracie would love to wear the latest fashions too, but on my pay, well, we could never afford it.

I'm close enough now to tip my hat. I have to say, they're pretty good-looking sorts, but they are rather heavy on the war paint. One pulls out a cigarette, lights up and leans on the fender, while the other three dash into the shop. I keep an eye on her. Women who smoke always look cheap to me.

The driver's door swings open and a bloke steps out dressed up like a politician on the take. The face under the fedora is doughy and cut-up, like he's taken too many knocks on the chin. His double-breasted pinstripe looks pretty flash, his shoes shine like mirrors and his get-up stands out like dog's balls. The only blokes out here who can afford to dress like that are the station owners when they go to the races. But this bloke has a broken nose and cauliflower ears. For all the flash clothes, he's no toff, this bloke. He looks like a pub brawler.

Flash sends me a look. I know the look; seen it too many times. It's the look people give to a copper when they hate his guts. I approach the smoking woman, who gives me the eye-over. I know that look too. It's the one crims gives you, when they're trying to tell you that they're not scared of you, *you copper mongrel.*

She doesn't appear sweet and innocent to me. I reckon you could strike a match on her face.

'Morning, madam,' I say to her, 'nice day to travel. Are you just visiting?'

She doesn't answer but draws hard on her cigarette, and looks over at the bloke. Flash comes up to me; looks like he's going to be doing the talking. He thinks he can stare me down. Good luck with that, mate. The girl gets nervous, stubs out her cigarette and hurries into Mayberry's.

'Morning,' I begin. 'Nice car you've got.'

'Yeah,' he replies. 'She's a beaut.'

Neither one of us is the slightest bit interested in the car.

'Taking the ladies shopping?' I ask. 'On your way through?'

He snorts. 'We're going to be working at the new dance hall.'

'Really?' I reply. He's shifting his weight uneasily. 'You mean, like a musical group?'

'Yeah, that's right. The girls are...singers, you know, like the Andrew Sisters. You heard of them?' he asks with a smirk.

'Of course I have.'

'We're here to entertain the troops. You know...' He stares at my stripes. 'We're helping the war effort, Sarge.'

'Sergeant Furey to you, sonny,' I reply angrily.

'Sergeant Furey,' he replies, pretending to be respectful.

'You're like a manager, are you?' I ask.

'I call myself an impress-air-ree-oh. Tommy Sharman's the name,' he tosses back. 'I manage singing acts and boxers in Sydney usually, but I thought I'd break these girls in, up here, in the north. We hear there are a lot of soldiers up this way needing entertainment. The girls are just starting out, but they have a lot of promise.'

'You're a long way from the big smoke. Got a name for them?' I ask. 'A stage name?'

'I'm still working on that,' he replies smoothly, 'but I like The Diamond Dolls.'

'Not bad.'

'I think it's got potential.' He smiles, but it's about as genuine as Mrs Jessop's glass-paste tiara.

'Got a place to stay?' I probe. 'You might find it a little difficult these days…'

'That's all been taken care of by the owners of the dance hall,' Sharman responds. I notice he's fidgeting with his hat.

'Oh, and who are they? I'm sure to know them,' I prod.

He looks a little too nervous. 'I really don't know who they are.'

I scoff. 'You don't know who's employed you? Come all this way? On what? A message from Our Lord? Don't give me that, of course, you do.' I edge closer to him and give him my cold stare.

Sharman starts to blink like a scared rabbit, but I'm not certain that he's actually afraid of me.

'You must know who's going to be paying you before you pack up the Buick and head north, mustn't you?'

'It's on the quiet. They don't want me to throw their names around too much, you know?' he mutters.

'Oh, I see. It's my job,' I say with a smile, 'when blow-ins come into my town, to know their business, especially if they're from the big smoke and they're connected to the…entertainment world.'

'You've got the wrong end of the stick, Sergeant Furey,' Sharman says defensively. 'We're not here to cause any trouble.'

'That's good to know. So, then, you won't mind telling me who's behind it and going to be running it,' I continue.

I realise too late that I've just handed him a weapon.

'Well, I'm surprised you don't already know, seeing as you're the top copper in this place.' Sharman's eye twitches.

'Don't get cheeky with me, son.' I square up to his ugly mug. 'Any more back chat from you, and I'll have you in the watch house.'

He's given up playing scared. 'Yeah? On what charge?'

'Haven't made my mind up, but I'll book you on something, don't you worry about that. You see, I can make your stay here as comfortable or as uncomfortable as I want. Which way do you want this to go?'

He takes off his hat, wipes his brow with a silk hanky, then takes a deep breath. 'I'd tell you,' he begins, 'except that I was supposed to keep all mum about this.'

'It's all right, I won't be flapping my gums.'

He's lowered his guard.

'Right, then… Your mayor invited us up here to entertain. Barry Jessop. He's setting up the dance hall.'

Now, that's interesting.

'So, Mayor Jessop, hey? He's bit of a dynamo.'

'But I'm not supposed to tell anyone that.' He fumbles for a cigarette out of his suit pocket and lights it.

'But I'm not anyone, am I?'

His eyes move from side to side. 'This is between you and me, right?'

I've unsettled him. He's pleading. 'Mum's the word.' I grin.

'We're just here to entertain the troops. The American troops, that is. We're not here to cause any trouble, like,' he adds. 'The dance hall is being set up for the Yanks. Just the Yanks.'

The girls come out of the dress shop dangling packages tied with string.

'I appreciate your honesty, Mr Sharman. I have no reason to detain you any further, so I'll let you go, then. Good day to you. Enjoy your stay, and keep out of trouble.' I glance at the girls. 'It must be expensive keeping these ladies dolled up. I hope the dance hall pays well.'

He doesn't reply, but takes a few deep breaths instead.

I wave goodbye as they get back into the car and the Buick pulls away, and then I head straight to the council offices.

CHAPTER SEVEN

'Sergeant Furey!'

Vera Anderson, the pinched-face, skinny clerk hisses at me from across the counter. 'You can't go in there. Mayor Jessop is involved in a very important meeting.'

Vera Anderson is always sour. I reckon it's because she's never had a bloke to take care of her. I don't actually know if she's ever had a bloke; I've never seen her with one. Now that she's in the twilight of her thirties, time is running out for her.

I reckon she would be a lot nicer to people if she had a bloke.

'This is important police business. I'm sure he won't mind if I duck in for a minute.' I'm forceful but polite.

'But you must know that this is highly inappropriate, Sergeant Furey,' she argues.

I've got better than things to do than stand around and listen to her prattling on.

'Excuse me,' I growl. I push on past her, and head down the corridor towards Jessop's office. She manages to dart ahead of me and knocks on his door first.

It doesn't open.

'You need to give it a good whack. Here, I'll give it a go.' I nudge her away and thump. After a while, the door flies open.

The mayor looks a little crimson in the face. 'What...on... earth...' he stumbles over his words. 'What...is the reason for this interruption? I'm preparing for a very important meeting. Miss Anderson, what is the meaning of this?'

I...I don't really know,' she stammers. 'The sergeant said it was vital that he see you, a police matter.'

'I won't take up much of your time,' I interrupt.

Jessop frowns. 'Can't you see I'm busy? Can't it wait?'

'No, it can't. Best if we talk inside. Where we can't be overheard. What I have to say is best kept between the two of us,' I reply.

I can tell he's worried. 'I have Colonel Reynolds coming in here soon on a critical matter,' he mumbles.

'Well, that's good. He can fill me in as well.'

Jessop's mouth drops open. As I brush past him, I feel like warning him to close it before he swallows a fly. He slams the door shut.

I sit down without invitation opposite his big wooden desk.

'This is highly inappropriate,' he bleats. 'I'll be contacting your superiors.'

I have no patience for nonsense. 'Sit down, Jessop, we need to talk.'

The thinning curls on the crown of his head spring up in spite of all the brilliantine trying to hold them down, and they jiggle as he speaks. He looks like a wet poodle.

He proclaims, 'Some respect, please! I'm the mayor of this town How dare you!'

I cross my legs. 'How about you sit down and tell me all about the new dance hall? I hear you're in it a lot deeper than you're letting on.' I want to laugh as Jessop goes from blustering blowfish to stunned mullet in an instant. 'Sit down!' I bark.

He returns to his desk and sits quietly but doesn't answer straight away. He looks like he's trying to find the words, the right ones, the ones that won't dig him in deeper. His mouth is flapping soundlessly.

I prompt him. 'I hear that you've put quite a few quid into this dance hall and that you expect to take quite a few out. And you were front-and-centre when the vote was taken, speaking up about its merits. Seems the only thing that you forgot to mention at the town meeting was that you were the one financing it. Got me to wondering: is that allowable in your position?'

'Yes... No... Well... Perhaps there was a misunderstanding about my role in it,' he begins, 'but this is war, and the rules have changed.' He lights up suddenly. 'I didn't want people thanking me personally for it. I think the troops deserve all the comforts of home.'

'Right. So, the dance hall's providing a service.'

He nods. 'A service to servicemen, you might say.'

'What I think you really mean is that you see a business opportunity in it,' I throw back, 'and you're cashing in. On the war...'

'Oh, no...' he begins. 'I wouldn't say that.'

I watch him quiver. 'I understand perfectly. Some people sacrifice their entire lives to fight wars, where others stay warm and dry, and reap the rewards.'

He sucks in air like a pair of bellows. 'How dare you! How dare you insinuate...'

'It's all right, whether you've done the right thing or not, I don't really care. If you want to get involved in dodgy business ventures,' I reply, 'go right ahead. But what I do care a lot about, is what will be happening in and around the dance hall.'

'Meaning what?'

I tell him about Mr Sharman and his troupe.

Jessop rolls his eyes. 'So what? They're just the entertainment, Furey. They're singers, come here all the way from Sydney.'

I shrug. 'And does that entertainment involve them lying on their backs and collecting a few quid at the end? You see, Jessop, what you call entertainment, I call pandering.'

'Oh, come on,' he replies indignantly, 'that's most presumptive of you. Just because they're singers, doesn't mean they are...professional women.'

'Prostitutes, you mean. I've seen my fair share of them and I'm not being presumptuous, Jessop, I'm being realistic. They don't look like singers to me.'

'For God sakes, they're the entertainment.' His eyes twitch more than a rabbit's whiskers. 'You were a soldier, you have to understand. Stop being a wowser, Furey. This town could do with a bit of livening up. It's been dead for far too long.'

'Which brings me to my next question…'

Without warning, the door opens and Colonel Reynolds marches in. He appears surprised that I'm with the mayor. He throws a glance at Jessop.

'Sergeant Furey.' The colonel shakes my hand. 'What a pleasant surprise. I'm still waiting for your next visit out to the base.'

And I'm still waiting for your invitation.

'I'll come by, once everyone settles in,' I return.

Jessop's eyes are flying between my face and Reynolds's. 'So you two know each other?'

He's put out, like a bloke who just spotted his wife out on the arm of another man.

'Comrades-in-arms. We fought in the same battle in the last war,' Reynolds replies.

And then just realised that the man he spotted her with is her brother.

'That's good then, Colonel,' Jessop continues. 'The sergeant was enquiring about the dance hall. You two can have a soldier-to-soldier talk and explain all the benefits.'

'You know about the dance hall?' Reynolds says with surprise. 'It was supposed to be kept under wraps until the grand opening. I don't want my boys finding out too soon. It might distract them from the job at hand.'

'But you don't have a business interest in this like the mayor?' I enquire.

'Of course not, Jack,' Reynolds replies, 'that would be highly improper. But the United States Air Force has provided some logistical support.'

'So, is this going to be open for all personnel?' I push.

Jessop shakes his head. 'Just Americans.'

'Really? And how do you reckon that'll go with the Australian personnel? My advice to you both is, don't do it.'

'Jack, the Australians have their own facilities, so I think we deserve ours,' Reynolds argues. 'Our boys should be allowed to have somewhere of their own. A reminder of home.'

'I'm sorry, Colonel, I have to disagree. The Australian canteens are open to everyone.' I can tell he's building a wall, even as I speak. 'Come on, this is our country, you blokes are the guests here.' I'm having trouble hiding my anger.

'I'm sorry it upsets you so, Jack,' he replies, 'but I think you're overreacting.'

'Fine. We'll see.'

'Well your boys will have to accept it, or our MPs will arrest them the minute they step out of line. Just remember, we're providing the bulk of the manpower and supplies, Jack. We deserve our comforts. Australians have to get used to how Americans do things.'

'Then you better get a lot more MPs in. Some of our blokes are coming back from the Middle East. They've just been fighting the Afrika Korps; they're tough soldiers. They won't be taking any bullshit from a mob of MPs. Good luck, trying to turn them away.'

'I tell you, you're overreacting, Jack, they'll be fine. There's plenty of entertainment for your boys elsewhere.'

He lays a hand on my shoulder, but I brush it away.

'You have to accept how we do things,' he continues. 'I accept that you're worried about peace and good governance, but the thing is, it's not peacetime. You're going to have to cut us some slack. This is war. It's different now.'

'So I keep bloody hearing. I tell you what, a seedy dance hall and a bunch of mattress commandoes to service your blokes in my town—I never thought I'd see the day.'

'They're not prostitutes,' Jessop interrupts.

'Right, they're singers. Pull the other one, Mayor Jessop, I didn't come down in the last bloody shower,' I growl as I uncross my legs, stand up and head to the door. 'You haven't heard the bloody last of this.'

'Everything is going to be all right,' Reynolds assures me as he follows me to the door. 'Come out to the base for a drink. Let's talk this through. We can sort this out between you and me, soldier to soldier.'

So, you think I can be bought for a beer and a steak.
'No thanks, Colonel. I've got to see a man about a dog.'
'What?'
'You work it out,' I reply.

CHAPTER EIGHT

As soon as I get back to the station, I get on the blower to the inspector in Townsville and tell him what's going on.

There's silence at the other end, so deafening that I enquire if he's still there.

To my great surprise, he also says I'm overreacting about the dance hall's potential to cause civil unrest. *Bloody hell!* He goes on to say that the Americans are entitled to run their own recreational facilities.

Then he hits me with a bombshell I wasn't expecting.

The long and short of it is that the Americans will be operating under their own law and procedures while they're in this country. In our country! There's a directive that's just come in from the Australian government: if the Americans break any laws here they are to be handled by their military courts. If I arrest one, I must immediately hand them over to their military police. That goes for Australian personnel also. They are to be handed over to their military police.

Bugger me dead, I think. *Where do my men and I stand?*

I can be candid with the inspector; he was an old army mate of mine, although I can never bring myself to call him by his name.

'Hang on, Inspector,' I reply sternly, 'you're saying that we're supposed to let the military take over our town? We're supposed to stand around like stale bottles of beer while they run amok?'

'Don't be stupid, Jack, you're still responsible for the civilians. The military won't have anything to do with them.'

'But what if a Yank kills or rapes a local? You're telling me that I go and arrest the culprit, but then I have to hand him straight over to the Yanks. That doesn't sound right to me. There won't be any justice, you've got to know that, not for the victim, anyway. What's the bet they'll be taking his side.'

'Now, now, Jack, calm down,' he says, 'they have laws to deal with that. They won't let them get away with it. They're our guests; they'll know to respect our laws.'

'We'll see,' I reply.

He steers me away. 'How are the missus and the young bloke doing? I should get out there for a visit.'

'They're fine, thanks. Haven't seen much of them lately, but no one's grumbling: they know I have an important job to do,' I respond.

'Maybe, you should take a break, Jack. I might be able to get someone to replace you for a few days, at least. You could come down to the coast, do a bit of fishing. You sound tired to me.'

'I'll be right; nothing that a beer won't fix.'

'You should take a bit of time off, anyway. You've hardly ever had a holiday.'

'I'll think about it,' I reply. 'Let's get through the military occupation first.'

'I could give you a desk job down here. It'd give you more time with the family.'

'I'll be right. I don't need any mollycoddling. You know, I'm not saying all these things because I'm a bit tired: it's past experience talking. The Poms tried the same sort of thing on us in France. It ended in fights. And you know what happened in the Middle East'

'I know, but it'll be all right, Jack,' he reassures me. 'The war will be over soon and everything will get back to normal.'

'That's what everyone thought the first time around, and that took four years to sort out. I'll keep you posted, Inspector.'

'I'm sure you will Jack,' he sighs, 'I'm sure you will.'

CHAPTER NINE

There's not much going on in town today, so I heed the inspector's advice and head home early to spend more time with Gracie and Mikey.

The boy's already back from school and out in the back yard, slapping a ball against the fence with his cricket bat. His face brightens up the minute he claps eyes on me.

'Dad!' he yells, 'Dad!'

He drops the bat and runs over to me and I tousle his hair.

'Come on,' he says. 'Come play with me.'

'Soon as I say g'day to your mum,' I reply.

I creep inside, while Mikey picks up where he left off.

Gracie's in the kitchen, humming to the radio, skinning a rabbit. She hasn't heard a thing. I hear the rip as she slips the knife down the rabbit's belly and slides her fingers under its skin.

She's a fine woman, my missus.

She hasn't said another word about adopting the foundling, but I know it hasn't left her mind. She has the patience of a saint, has my Gracie, as well as the determination of a mule. We never would have had Mikey otherwise. We tried to have kids for a long time, but she kept losing the baby. We were both beside ourselves with grief, but it hit Gracie especially hard. At one point, I thought she would have a nervous breakdown. She went from tears at dawn, to silence and staying in bed all day. The local doctor wasn't much help; he wanted to put her in some madhouse. I let him know quick-smart that that wasn't on.

A friend of hers told her it was her own fault for doing too much, so she tried doing nothing. She ate raw liver and drank stout so she could be strong, and she would have spent the whole nine months standing on her head, if she'd thought it would help. But no matter what she did, it all ended the same way.

Gracie said one day that we were cursed. She'd heard of such things.

So we went to see Father Donnelly. He said he didn't believe in curses or fairies, and he told us that miracles happen in Ireland all the time. I said it was a very long way to go from here to there. I told him that if we'd had the money, we would have already gone to Mayo, to Croagh Patrick, and climbed to the summit on our knees, all two thousand, five hundred feet of it. We were that desperate for a baby.

But we didn't.

Instead, Father Donnelly told us that we had to say the rosary every day in front of Our Lady until Gracie became pregnant. Gracie said once might not be enough, there were an awful lot of people doing an awful lot of praying and we needed to be heard above them, so she said it three times a day. And for the rest of the time...well... You know what I mean.

Thank the Lord, within six months Gracie was pregnant again. Then we worried about her having another miscarriage, so we kept up the rosaries. We couldn't lose another; it would have been the end of us. So we kept it up religiously, until, a dozen years ago, Michael Joseph was born.

He was a beautiful blessing from God.

Gracie went into labour while we were at Mass. Father Donnelly finished the Eucharist, hurried through the blessing, and rushed us to the hospital in his car. He was in such a flap, that I was certain we'd crash. He crossed himself before every intersection, flew through them, and we didn't. And now I have my precious family.

There's nothing I wouldn't do for them.

I watch Gracie rinse off the rabbit and decide I should spend more time with her and the boy. I sneak up, put my arms around her waist and she starts. A quick kiss and then I trot back outside.

Boys need their fathers.

'Is Mikey the next Don Bradman?' Gracie smiles as she comes out of the back door with a tray of drinks.

'He's going to be better than the Don, aren't you, son?' I reply, and Mikey grins.

I'm bowling some good leg spinners to him, which he tips off to either side. He could take a swing at them, but he knows it'd make an easy catch in the outfield. We don't have an outfield here, of course, but he's always thinking bigger and better. There's not much this child can't do well. He's a true all-rounder.

Gracie and I are proud as peacocks.

'Come on, I've got drinks for the Australian team.' She laughs as she puts the tray down on a table under the big mango tree.

A long time ago Gracie planted a choko vine beside the thunder-box to take care of the odours, and Mikey deals with the last ball of the over by nearly tearing the choko from its roots. I check it's still intact as I pick up the ball and catch the smell of the outhouse.

I've told them that one day we'll have a flushing indoor toilet, just like the ones they have in posh houses in the city. Meanwhile, Mikey's standing by the table, gulping his sarsaparilla. Gracie hands me a Melbourne Bitter and sips her shandy in the shade. Even when beer is in short supply, I know a publican who owes me favours. I look around me. Life is pretty near perfect. I know we could raise the foundling if she survives her ordeal, although I haven't changed my mind on the issue. Call me selfish, but I don't want to upset the applecart.

'Homework now,' says Gracie.

Mikey complains.

'Don't whine, Michael Joseph, it doesn't become you,' she scolds. 'We're after top of the class this term, not second.'

He looks to me for support, but I let him down with a shrug.

She says she'll let him play for another five minutes but no more, and he goes back to hitting the ball against the fence.

I get her another shandy and a beer for myself, and she tells me that she's seen the colonel at last and he isn't a bad sort, but not nearly as good looking as Gary Cooper. And he certainly isn't as handsome as me.

I kiss her on the cheek.

Her eyes are all over me; she's reading me like a book. 'Everything going all right, Jack?' she asks as she touches my knee.

'Right as rain,' I reply softly.

'Are you sure, love?'

'Working too hard. I'll be glad when this war's over.'

'Well, you could always ask for a different posting. You've been here long enough. And you're having more of those nightmares again.'

I lie, 'Really? I don't remember anything.'

She looks at her glass and not at me. 'You woke up screaming the other night. Even Mikey heard it.'

'I didn't realise it was that bad. I'm sorry, love,' I reply.

I can't tell her that I'd give anything not to remember what I've seen. Anything. During the day, I'm too busy to think about the war but at night, I'm back in the trenches. And there's more than that besides: the things I've seen since then. In my job, you try hard not to gather memories, but they stay in your head anyway. At night, when the rest of the world is still, in my soul there's turmoil.

Gracie says that perhaps it might help if I read a book before bed. She reckons it might take my mind off things. I don't know about reading before bed, although listening to music sometimes seems to help a bit.

'Would talking about it help, love?'

I feel a tear in my eye and pretend it's a bit of dirt. My dad would have given me a hiding with his belt if he'd seen me cry; *boys don't cry.* He was married to that belt, thick as the sole of his boot and twice as tough. He gave out lashes to us for nothing, even to my mum, reserving the bite of his buckle for the worst offences. Nearly took Mum's eye out with that buckle. I'm glad that Mikey never knew him.

May he rot in hell.

In my family, I've replaced the belt with hugs.

'My poor love,' Gracie says as she pats me on the shoulder.

'I'll sleep in the shed, so you and Mikey get some peace.'

'No, love. My husband sleeps beside me.' She stops to think for a while. 'We could talk to Father Donnelly. He'll be able to help.'

I wonder what a priest can do about it. 'I don't think even Father Donnelly could remove these memories from my mind.'

'Well, he helped bring us Mikey, didn't he?'

I can't fault her logic, so I go inside and try to talk to Mikey about history, but he tells me he's learned about it already.

After dinner, as I dry the dishes I say, 'You and Mikey are the greatest things that ever happened to me. I'll do everything in my power to make sure the both of you are happy.'

'Without Mikey and you,' says Gracie, 'I'd be... Well, I don't where I'd be.'

I lean over and kiss her on the forehead.

She's a fine woman, my missus.

CHAPTER TEN

Everyone's on leave today. Nobody asked me my thoughts on the matter, but if they had, I'd have told the brass they'd be mad to give the Americans and the Australian servicemen leave at the same time. They wouldn't have listened to a small town coppers anyway. Military brass knows it all. Full of piss and vinegar, as far as I can tell.

Nothing bloody changes. Bunch of dills.

My boys and I are prepared. The only saving grace is that the black servicemen won't be having their leave in Wangamba. It seems that the Americans don't want their white boys mixing with them, so they're taking them to a nearby town called Charlie's Creek instead. Charlie's Creek is a desert. It makes Wangamba seem like Sydney.

The first men to hit town are the ground crew and pilots from the RAAF: I count at least fifty of them, looking for trouble. The pubs are opening as they drive down the street. Right on time. Thirsty soldiers mean a lot of money in the till. The publicans have shipped in more grog and they've employed more staff, but I wonder if they've factored in any damage.

Our boys are off the trucks and into the public bar like a mob of eager cattle dogs. Before long, glasses in hand, they're spilling out onto the footpath. They're loud, and I'd sooner they kept their drinking inside the pub, but Dora Green's out from behind the bar and collecting the glasses as soon as they empty, so I cut them some slack.

Soon enough, they move along to the next pub, and we head that way too, just as a bunch of well-fed Australian MPs pull up beside us, ready to grind their axe in public. I've got their measure: you can see the pleasure they feel, shoving around the real soldiers. It's written in bold on each of their faces. Not one of them has seen a moment of combat, yet they'll all be the ones big-noting themselves after this war's over to anyone who'll listen.

I ask myself if we're the same, the police and the MPs. There's a big difference between what we do and what they do: we're all about upholding the law and they're all about bullying.

I watch their chests swell as they eye off the fliers, and I can see them thinking that the job that they do is somehow more important than that of our pilots. It brings to mind the night that some of the Diggers on the ship home from France grew so sick of the MPs, that they threw two of them overboard in the middle of the Indian Ocean, never to be seen again.

Perhaps I should tell them the story as a warning.

I'm still mulling that one over, when one of them opens the passenger door and hops out, glaring at me and stroking his truncheon. I find it disturbing.

He smirks as he says, 'There won't be any trouble around here today, so you might as well have the day off, Sarge.'

I turn my death stare on him. 'Is that so, Corporal? Well, here's hoping you're right.'

His mate pops out beside him, just for good measure.

'We'll be taking care of everything around here,' he snarls.

'Who? You?' I put my hands on my hips. 'Well, the Yanks might have a bit to say about that. Didn't anyone brief you? The Yanks are running the show now. Looks like you'll be answering to them.'

The corporal's taken aback. I've put a pin to his balloon.

Bugger him.

'And just a reminder, Corporal,' I continue, 'I am still the law in

Wangamba, and you'll address me as Sergeant Furey. Do I make myself clear?'

He laughs.

Smug bastard, this one is. I slide myself forward, until we're nearly nose to nose. 'I would have liked us to cooperate with each other, but apparently you have a problem with that. Just so you know, if you lay a finger on a single civilian, you'll wish you'd never put on that uniform, son.' I turn to his mate. 'And that goes for you, too. Good day.'

I continue my patrol along the street. There are only a few locals doing their shopping; most of them must have stayed home, but there's a steady stream of excited girls, dressed to the nines, all heading my way. As I stroll past the Swing Time Dancehall with its new sign (*American Personnel Only*), three jeeps with American MPs on board speed down the street and pull up. The girls stop dead and watch.

Two staff cars stop in front of the Jeeps, and their doors fly open. Reynolds gets out first.

He notices me and signals. 'We're about to open the Swing Time, Jack!' he yells. 'Come in for a visit once it's set up. There's a great band, plenty to eat and drink.'

He spots my confusion.

'As my guest,' he continues, 'you'll be an honorary American, Jack.'

'I'm afraid I can't, Colonel!' I yell back. 'I've got to keep an eye on the town.'

'It's going to be fine, Jack!'

I wave. 'Maybe later!'

Just then, a convoy of American trucks full of servicemen rattle down the street. Half of them are leaning out and they're all calling out to the girls and wolf whistling. Some of the girls call back, while others just stand there and giggle. One's already flashing them a glimpse of her thigh, and I can see trouble ahead.

The trucks come to a stop in front of the dance-hall door, and about a hundred blokes pile out. They're as excited as sheep let out of the yard, but the MPs push them back into line, snapping at their heels like kelpies. They build a human wall between the men and the girls while I stand around like a stale bottle of piss.

This doesn't feel like my town anymore.

The band strikes up in the dance hall and the music spills out onto the street. It's not my cup of tea. A few of our boys poke their heads out of the pub to take a look at the commotion. I watch the American MPs eyeing them off, and say a silent prayer, but it seems that our boys are content for the time being just to get some grog under their belts.

As I head back to the station, I stumble over Snowy parading around in his air raid uniform and his helmet like the boss cocky. He's appointed himself the town's Winston Churchill.

'Expecting any bombs, tonight?' I ask him. 'Have you spotted any Jap planes on the horizon?'

'It's not a joke, Sergeant Furey,' he snaps at me. 'It could happen at any time. We have to be ready.'

Without a wife, he has nothing better to occupy his hours. I'm thinking that perhaps I should introduce him to Vera Anderson.

I ask, 'No correction to do today then, Snowy?'

He puts on his best schoolmaster frown. He's recently cultivated a BBC accent, and it's always good for a laugh. 'The children can afford to wait for me to mark their homework. Unlike others, I prefer to take my civic duties seriously,' he chimes, 'and keep my eyes on the skies.'

'Well, can you let me know when they're coming?'

He huffs. 'I have no time for such frivolity, Sergeant. We're at war, you know.'

Now he's got my goat. Unlike Snowy, war and I have had intimate relations. 'I know what war looks, sounds, smells and tastes like, Snowy, even though you don't. I had nearly four years of it. You really don't have to remind me.'

He turns and marches away.

Back at my desk, I shuffle some paperwork as I have a cup of tea and think about the pointlessness of my job. I felt a little jealous of the MPs today, I'll admit it. There's something about the camaraderie of warriors that I miss. The MPs had it all in hand,

and I have to concede, with no leads on the foundling case and the servicemen behaving themselves so far, there isn't much for me to do here. So I imagine myself back in the army. I know that Gracie wouldn't like it, but at my age I wouldn't be sent into combat. I'd probably get in as an instructor in a training camp down south.

I'm not too old to join up again, am I?

I'm stuck on that thought when Mahoney bursts through the front door like a scrubber bull charging out of the bush.

'The Australian trucks are on their way. I could see them from the top of the street,' he pants.

I stand up and grab my cap and we head out. By the time Mahoney and I reach the dance hall, Higgins is already there. The windows are covered so we can't see in. The girls have disappeared from the street, and I assume they've joined the American servicemen inside.

The trucks crawl past the dance hall, and the Diggers spot it and start shouting and whooping. They're still dressed in their desert kit; they're lean and tanned from the unrelenting North African sun. The battle's still written all over their faces. And judging from their faces, it was bloody hard.

The trucks pass the Swing Time and drop the men at the other end of the street.

Bloody fools. That's not going to stop them heading up this way.

Out front, the American MPs have also noticed them. They suddenly look agitated. One of them takes out his pistol from his hip holster and checks the action. Another one taps his palm with his truncheon.

I turn to face them. 'I'd put the guns away if I were you, boys. This isn't the Wild West.'

One of the MPs sniggers and it riles me. He's a Southerner.

'We don't want no trouble neither, Sergeant,' he drawls.

'Then let me talk to them when they get here,' I suggest. 'They might listen to me.'

'This is our dance hall,' he continues. 'We know how to handle ourselves against this bunch of hounds.'

I'm shaking my head. 'In case you didn't know, this bunch of hounds—as you call them—have just defeated the Afrika Korps at El Alamein. They're seasoned fighters and they're on home soil. Don't believe for a minute that they're going to be afraid of you blokes. Unless you want this place destroyed, I suggest you let them in.'

The first MP whispers to another, and then disappears inside. Moments later, Reynolds wanders out.

'Everything in order?' he asks one of the MPs.

'The Australians have arrived, sir!' he replies.

'Well, you know what to do,' Reynolds says. 'This is our dance hall and you're here to uphold military law. This dance hall is American territory. Defend it.'

'Colonel Reynolds,' I butt in. 'May I have a private word?' I draw him aside. 'We're both straight-talkers, Colonel, and you know I have everyone's best interests at heart.' I pause and he looks bored. 'Don't be bloody stupid, let our boys in, Colonel. They won't cause any trouble. Treat them with respect and I promise they'll behave themselves.'

I watch him grow crimson. 'This is not your call, Furey. Stay out of it, or the next call I make will be to your superior. You appear to have forgotten the chain of command. I'm the officer. I'm in charge of this situation.'

I'm struck dumb for a second. *You're pulling rank?* It irks me but I don't bat an eyelid. 'Then you'll be cleaning up the bloody mess. And if any civilians are hurt, you can bet I'll be the one making the enquiries.'

He steps away. 'Good day, Sergeant Furey,' he growls.

I shake my head and walk off, gesturing at Mahoney and Higgins to follow. The bugger's been trying to butter me up from the moment we met. Since I haven't wasted any emotion on him, it doesn't matter the least what he thinks of me. I always suspected there was no sincerity behind Reynolds's flattery.

I spot dozens upon dozens of Australian soldiers coming up from the other end of the street. The fliers are still working their way down the hill, one pub at a time, and they cheer as the Diggers pass by. I can tell from their war-weary faces that they have their blood up.

The Diggers and the Scots. The angriest soldiers I've ever known.

I can just tell by the way they look and the purpose in their stride, that the Diggers already know about the dance hall restrictions. They're primed and ready to go. Someone's worded them up. The Australian MPs limp along beside them, clueless, and they're about as useless as eunuchs in a brothel.

I signal my constables to stop, and we try to make a barrier between the Diggers and the dance hall. Leading the approaching contingent are two sergeants. They're not interested in curbing the behaviour of the other Diggers.

I step forward. 'I'm Sergeant Furey!' I shout. The stone buildings either side of me catch my voice and I'm bloody loud. 'I'm ex-AIF. I served in France in the last war. Where are your officers?' I ask.

'Where do you reckon they are? In the bloody officers' mess, having a good time,' one of the sergeants replies, his lip curling. He's a big muscular man, over six feet. I'm giving away inches in both height and reach. I wouldn't want to tangle with him in a fight.

'Those bludgers are having a good time and we've been told the Yanks think they run this town.'

'I wouldn't worry about it.' I try to reason with him, 'There are other places you can go to for a good time. You fellas should try the cinema or one of the pubs. They'll look after you.'

'Fuck that. We want to go into the dance hall and meet some sheilas!' he yells back at me. 'You might be happy the Yanks have taken over, but we're not going to bloody stand for it, all right? This is our bloody country, and we're going to do something about it.'

All around him, the Diggers wave their fists and cheer. They push past us. Now they've turned into an unruly mob. The Australian MPs have finally realised that they need to do something quick, so they take out their truncheons, stand shoulder to shoulder and try to block their progress. A couple of locals dive in to help them

'Halt! You are not to continue any further! If you do, you'll be disobeying a military direction!' one of them bellows.

The sergeant bristles. 'You can stick your military direction, bludger. Where were you bastards when we were at El Alamein?

You can go to buggery, you bludging bastard!' He drops the MP onto the footpath with a single punch to the jaw. The other MPs break rank and start swinging their truncheons, but within a few seconds, they're all laid out like skittles.

The Diggers push on towards the Swing Time, while the boys and I follow in their wake. I keep trying to talk the sergeant down, but the crowd drowns me out.

They're nearly at the door of the dance hall.

'Come on, men,' I hear myself say, 'this isn't the way to solve it.'

The sergeant snaps, 'This is the only way we know. Go home, Sergeant Furey. We'll sort this out.'

'Don't disgrace the reputation we've built!'

He spins around and I'm expecting a punch. Instead, he says, 'My dad was in the last war. I know what you blokes did. You weren't angels: you never let the bloody poms push you around.'

'But it will go on your record, son. I'm directing you to stop, or I'll have to arrest you.'

'Bugger off and stick to handing out fines for littering.' The sergeant laughs as he pushes me away, and I stumble backwards.

Higgins props me up. 'Mahoney,' I say, 'get back to the station and get on the blower. Call the base. Tell them to send their officers and reinforcements, immediately.'

Mahoney runs down the street as fast as he can.

I right myself. 'Clear the street of any civilians, Higgins!'

He also takes off, blowing his whistle as he runs, flapping his arms and ordering the locals off the street. Further along, Snowy grasps the wrong end again, and I hear his whistle screech as he directs servicemen and civilians alike into the bomb shelter.

It's not an air raid, you bloody fool!

I trail along to the dance hall, even though I don't have the faintest idea what I'm going to do once I get there. The Yanks have put up a wooden barricade near the entry and their MPs are now lined up behind it, pistols drawn. I recognise Corporal Hoffman instantly.

The sergeant's so angry that the veins in his neck stick out. 'Let us in, you Yankee bastards,' he roars, 'or cop a fucking flogging.'

'This is American territory. You are not American servicemen.

You are not permitted in here,' Hoffman replies. He lifts his pistol above his head and fires a shot.

You're trying to douse a fire with petrol, you idiot!

The Australians aren't armed, yet not one of them retreats. A few of them pull their belts off and wrap the heavy webbing tight around their hands, and point the hard brass buckles forward. Others hold them like slingshots.

I know what's coming, and I also know the best I can do right now is duck down behind a car. If I retreat, I might cop a bullet. They're all beyond reason. I watch the Diggers run at the barricade and I hear the ping of bullets aimed lower.

'Halt or I'll fire straight at you!' Hoffman's voice is breaking. All of the MPs have their pistols aimed square at the Diggers. I look for Reynolds, but he's AWOL, tucked up safely inside with the others, no doubt. Meanwhile, there's a war happening right here.

The music has stopped, and the dance hall's door is ajar. Some of the servicemen and a handful of girls press forward. They seem to think it's a show, giggling until one of the Diggers picks up a rubbish bin and another pulls a street sign out of the footpath and holds it up like a spear. The MPs are wide-eyed—both theirs and ours. They know they're heavily outnumbered. The Diggers are going to tear them apart like a pack of wild dogs when they get their hands on them.

The rubbish bin flies straight at the MPs, as the bloke with the sign swings it at them. They knock down three Yanks. A second bin crashes through the window and glass scatters everywhere.

After that, it's chaos. The girls scream, jostling to get back inside as the shooting starts. *Bam, bam, bam*: three shots fired in rapid succession, and I throw myself on the ground. There's lot of yelling, more screams, men crying out in pain, others swearing, the thump of boots running, crunching glass. I peer over the car's bonnet. Two of the Diggers are down: one's wounded in the leg and the other's hit in the arm. They're awake and an army medic is already tending to them. I hear someone groaning behind me. I turn my head and spot Snowy writhing and yelping.

'Help me!' he whimpers through his tears. 'Sergeant!'

I crawl over and check him. There's a trickle of blood past his left eye. It's decent enough, I suppose, to the uninitiated.

Snowy's hysterical. 'I'm almost blind! Everything's turning black!' He places his hand on my arm. 'I never thought it would end this way!'

I pull out my hanky and throw it to him. 'Here, wipe your face with this and pull yourself together!'

He coughs. 'Am I dying?'

I want to laugh. 'For Christ sakes, it's only a shrapnel wound, barely an inch long. Stop moaning like a bloody girl.'

I leave him in the throes of death and go over to help the medic, sniggering at the thought of the tale Snowy will spin in an effort to get a war pension and a campaign medal out of it. Meanwhile, the medic's arm is up and he's yelling for an ambulance.

Higgins is sprinting back towards me. 'Ring for an ambulance!' I shout.

The Yanks are in retreat, holed up in the dance hall. The Diggers have moved back too, although the sergeant's still trying to fire them up.

'Let's break in, boys,' he shouts, 'and do them over!'

Enough is enough.

I walk up to him.

'Piss off, copper bastard,' he says as he tries to push me away.

I'm not going anywhere.

'You are a disgrace to the Australian uniform, lad.' As the ruckus settles, my voice booms. 'Even worse than that, you've messed up my town and scared the locals. You are a dead set, bloody drongo. It's just a bloody dance hall. Who bloody cares about a dance hall? Look around at what's happened: good men are wounded. You're wasting all this effort fighting an ally, and meanwhile the enemy's laughing as he walks right in and rapes your mothers and sisters. All while you're busy arguing amongst yourselves.'

He's shaking his head. 'I haven't spotted any Japs, Huns or Eyeties around here, only Yanks, as far as I can see. Maybe they're the ones doing the raping. Maybe you want to turn a blind eye to them an' maybe you even make money off of them. But I don't.'

I can feel my jaw tighten. 'You,' I growl, 'will all move away from the area, immediately!'

He lifts his chin. He's still posturing for a fight.

I suck in some air and breathe it out. 'Really,' I say. He's too dumb for words. 'Well then, cop this!' I drop him with a sharp upper cut to the chin. He falls like a bag of cement and lies on the footpath, unconscious. Most of the others look uncertain but, just in case, I whip my truncheon out.

'Move away, I said or I'll be knocking some more heads in!' I shout.

While they mull it over, Mahoney arrives with his truncheon out, and they start to dawdle away from the dance hall. In the distance, some more Australian MPs arrive.

Where were you lazy bastards when this was happening? Thank God for country coppers. We've got it all under control.

I can still hear Snowy moaning in the background.

'Shut the whingeing, Snowy or I'll give you a dose of this.' I show him my truncheon. 'After the day I've had so far, I tell you what, I'll be happy to get rid of your pain.'

Mahoney is toeing the sergeant with his boot. 'What happened to him?'

'He fell over, clumsy bugger,' I reply.

He smiles. 'Well, I suppose he'll just have to be more careful in future, Sergeant Furey.'

CHAPTER ELEVEN

Today, I heard that the foundling died.

She was barely alive when I last saw her, and it was either a miracle or a tragedy that she survived as long as she did: you take your pick. Once she got to the hospital, she never left there. At first she was weak and dehydrated, and the sister fed her through the night, and she seemed to do better. Then Doc McDonald said that she developed whooping cough in her last few days. She simply never had a chance.

God rest her tiny soul.

The mother—whoever she is—isn't just guilty of criminal neglect anymore. The crime she's committed is far worse: she's damned her immortal soul. I feel no sympathy for her. I rarely do.

But it's not the baby's death that troubles me the most. I haven't had any clues as to the mother's identity, and it's possible that I never will. The truth is that some crimes—a lot of crimes—are never solved. The baby's likely to go nameless and unmourned into a pauper's grave. At least, since she was born and had a life, however short, she'll have a burial. Unlike ours.

I'm sitting at my desk, looking out past the door and wondering how I'm going to break the news to Gracie.

I know she's been holding out hope that the baby would be fine, and that we could raise her as our own. She mentioned it once or twice, even though I've tried to tell her she was on a fool's errand, but she wouldn't listen. Once Gracie has something fixed in her mind, she never listens. She shuts out logic and I'm powerless to persuade her. So I usually say nothing.

Constable Mahoney says he's heard that Father Donnelly went to the hospital to christen the baby. He's heard the baby was named *Mabelle. Ma belle, ma belle amie*: phrases I brought back with me from the Great War, and I've mentioned them at home from time to time. Even though she never said so, I suspect Gracie's behind the choice of name, and that she most likely stood up as Mabelle's sponsor.

Perhaps that's not such a bad thing, since Mabelle has no surname. She has no family to cry for her.

I'm not relishing the thought of telling Gracie, and I'm still hanging onto that thought when she dashes in. I catch sight of her rushing through the door and, as much as I love to see her, my heart sinks. I can tell from the red rings around her eyes that she knows.

'Oh, Jack,' she says, 'is it true?'

'Yes dear,' I reply. 'I heard about it not long ago from Doc McDonald, but how did you find out so soon?'

'The hospital called me directly.' She's frowning.

I don't know what to say. If I ask her if she's all right, it's as if I'm thinking she won't be.

She straightens her skirt and fidgets with her bag. At last she says, 'I can tell you're worried about me.'

'And should I be?'

'No, no, it's all right. I won't say I'm fine, but it's different from when...well you know... I'm sad, of course, but I did try to listen when you said she wouldn't be ours. I did try...' The tears are gathering in her eyes.

'I'm sorry, love.' I give her a hug. 'I wish it had ended differently. The best I can do for Mabelle now is to try to find her mother.'

'Yes, do. She has to learn a lesson. It is not acceptable to abandon your child, no matter what.'

‘Of course not. She let her baby die, and I’m afraid that she’s going to have to pay for it,’ I assure her and it seems to help. ‘If the mother’s not made an example of, what with all the soldiers about and a town full of apparently willing women, there could well be a spate of similar things happening.’

Gracie nods. ‘We may be at war,’ she says, ‘but morals are morals.’ She takes a hanky from her bag, wipes her eyes and blows her nose. She pecks me on the cheek. ‘If it’s all right with you, I’ll arrange for her burial.’

‘If it’s all right with the Doc and Father Donnelly, it’s fine by me.’

I watch her sigh as she leaves, and I’m as proud of her as I can be.

CHAPTER TWELVE

Gracie's up at dawn and the sound of her nightgown brushing past the foot of the bed wakes me up. I watch her dress through my half-shut eyes. She pulls off her nightgown and stands there for a while. She's still a sight to behold. After that, it's knickers and bra. She lifts her suspender belt off the chair and hooks it around her waist, sits down and starts to pull on her right stocking.

'Bother!' she says.

'What's wrong, darl?'

She looks over. 'Sorry, love,' she replies, 'I didn't mean to wake you up.' She lifts the stocking up to the beam of sunlight sneaking in between the curtains, and she sighs. 'Well, that's that. My last good pair have finally given up the ghost.' She takes off her suspender belt again, pulls on her slip and then her dress. 'Some of the women have gone back to wearing socks. I didn't want to be one of them, but...'

'Never mind, love. It's just a bit of vanity. You'll look sweet in socks.'

'I know it's just a bit of vanity. I know I shouldn't pine over it.' She makes balls out of her stockings and throws them in the drawer. 'I'll take my vanity to the confessional.'

I smile. That's the worst sin my Gracie has to confess and I'm a lucky man. I sit up and toss my legs over the side of the bed and wince. I'm still on the right side of fifty, but my knees haven't been the same since France. I can't let the pain show.

Over breakfast, she tells me she's been thinking about Mabelle's mother. 'I went to bed with her in my mind last night,' she says, 'and I thought of something in the wee hours. That's when things come to me, you know. The wee hours are almost as good as taking a bath for remembering things you've forgotten.'

'Oh yes,' I reply, spreading a thin paste of dripping over my bread and sipping my tea.

'Well, there is a girl…at church… Although she's a bit young…'

'Go on.' I cool my scalded tongue on the dripping until it melts away.

'Bernadette Douglas.'

'Minnie and Bert Douglas's daughter? But she's barely fifteen, isn't she? Whatever brought her to mind?'

'Sixteen,' she replies, 'and God forgive me for what I'm about to say. You see, I noticed the poor dear was getting rather chubby earlier this year, and I happened to mention it to Minnie one day after Mass. Not in a spiteful way, mind: just out of concern. The thing was, Minnie took it particularly badly. She told me straight out that it was none of my business. After that, Bernadette never came to Mass again. Minnie, Bert and the younger ones did, but not Bernadette. Still hasn't. Now I think of it, she was wearing an awful lot of clothes on a warm day.' She looks worried. 'That's not idle gossip, is it?'

I reply, 'I absolve you of your sin.'

She looks shocked. 'That's not your power to do,' she says, and I feel sheepish.

CHAPTER THIRTEEN

After the riot, the dance hall shut down for a few weeks. I wrote a thorough report for Inspector Bower, except that the bit where I dropped the sergeant on his arse missed the final draft. Apparently my quick actions and initiative were noted, but beyond that there was silence. The dance hall's since reopened. It seems it's all done and dusted.

I don't know if anyone was charged. I heard the wounded blokes recovered, and the Diggers were confined to base until they moved up north for jungle training. When they were eventually given leave, the Americans relented and let them in.

And there were no incidents.

I haven't seen Colonel Reynolds around at all. For all I know, he may have gone elsewhere. Just as well: he's done his dash with me.

The town's certainly changed. I'll wager there'll be a few girls nursing broken hearts once the Yanks leave. Every night Gracie's full of stories about which of the local ladies have taken up with the Americans, and every morning I do my best to forget it. Jesus might have been above judging others, but I'm not, so it's probably best I don't know. We've all heard it: the Americans might be overpaid and over here, but I'm making it my mission to put a dampener on the oversexed.

Constable Mahoney said he caught a couple in the act in Downey's Lane, off the main street. He heard voices and stumbled across a Yank giving a woman a knee-trembler up against the wall. He thought it sounded like they were having a fight, so he had his truncheon drawn, but it turned out to be anything but. All I'll say is, Vera Anderson's looking pretty happy with herself lately and she's got a spring in her step.

Today I'm alone in the station, happy enough with the boredom that surrounds me, when the door creaks. I can't help scowling when I spot who's walking through it. Maud Percy. From our church. Self-appointed, self-righteous and self-important. I can tell by the twist of her mouth that she's on another one of her heavenly missions.

'Sergeant Furey!'

I duck under the desk.

'Sergeant, I need to speak to you on a most serious matter.'

I don't get up.

'I see you there,' she hisses, leaning over and tapping the counter with a bony finger.

She has a direct line to the Pope and God, so what could she possibly want with me?

'Really, Sergeant! I must insist!'

It's pointless hiding. I get up slowly, pretending I was tying a shoelace.

I flash her a look. 'Oh, it's you, Mrs Percy.'

She's apoplectic, and I know exactly why.

'Miss Percy!' she squawks. 'It's Miss Percy. You know very well!'

Of course I do. I'm winding her up. Old Maud would have to be the biggest gossip in town.

'Can we speak in private, Sergeant?'

'Of course.' She's knocked the wind out of me. There's no one here. Still, I lead her around the back.

She perches on the chair like a hawk. 'Have you seen her?' she snaps.

'Who, Miss Percy?'

'That horrible woman. The...the...abortionist... That murderer of human life!' She draws breath only when she finishes her sentence.

She's flushed. For a moment, I hope she'll pass out.

'Who? Floss McCarthy?' I respond. 'Last I heard she'd left after you led the campaign to run her out of town. That must have been five years ago.'

She interrupts, 'Yes, yes, of course. And that's only because Father Donnelly and I were doing God's good work. With no help from the police, I must say.'

She looks me over like one of the nuns who taught me in early primary school.

'Now, now, Miss Percy, there wasn't enough to prove that she was doing abortions. No one said she did, remember? I can't charge a person just based on suspicion. We're not in the Dark Ages anymore.'

'She must have been guilty, or else why would she have left town?'

I roll my eyes. 'She left,' I begin, 'because you turned her into a pariah and someone burned her house down. She left because she was scared out of her wits.'

'This is not the time for the whys and the wherefores. She's back again. What are you going to do about it?'

'Nothing. She's allowed to move back, if she wants to. It's a free country.'

'I must insist you visit her and find out what she is doing here,' she continues.

I pause before saying, 'I won't be doing that.'

'Well, Father Donnelly may have something to say about that!' she snaps back. 'You should know by now, you shouldn't get on the wrong side of Father Donnelly. The members of the Roman Catholic Church are the saviours of Christianity, unlike those idolatrous, heretic Protestants.' She's almost screeching. 'If you regard yourself as a good Catholic, you must believe, above all else, that all human life is precious. *Thou Shalt Not Kill, said the Lord*. Therefore, you must arrest her and punish her!' She's booming like she's preaching from the pulpit.

My mind flips to something I read once, about a man in France: Alfred Dreyfus, his name was.

I say, 'I also have to uphold the law of this state, and I can't go and arrest someone on your say-so. It's civil law before canon law around here. You'll find that even the church stopped burning witches without good cause a long, long time ago.'

She's turning crimson. 'Well, if you do not, I'll be speaking to Father Donnelly.'

The truth is, no Catholic in town wants to incur the wrath of Father Donnelly. He's fire and brimstone. And I certainly don't want to incur Gracie's displeasure for getting on the wrong side of the priest. She worships him.

I'm caught. 'Right. I'll go and have a talk to her, but that's all I can do.'

She gives me Floss's address and smirks. I don't really want to know how she found it out. I watch her leave; there's not an ounce of Christian compassion in her twisted old body. Then I lock up the station and head off.

God, give me strength.

Floss McCarthy answers the door as if she's expecting me.

She eyes me up and down and scowls. 'I was wondering when you'd come around. I can guess why you're here. I saw that old papist witch when I was buying groceries. So, she ran straight to you.' She shakes her head. 'You Papists like to stick together and tell each other stories about horrible sinners like me, just so you can feel better about yourselves.'

She's aged a lot since I last saw her; her hair is totally grey and she walks with a stick. For years she brought babies into the world as a midwife, but when all of this abortion stuff blew up she was struck off the register.

'I'm only here to check everything's all right,' I reply, 'as a policeman, and nothing else.'

'Hah! Well, there's nothing to see here, Jack.'

'I hope so, Floss. It didn't end well the last time.'

'Let's be perfectly frank about why you're here, shall we? You've popped in to check if everything's all right—as you say—because you think I'm setting up an abortion clinic, don't you?'

'Are you?' Even in wartime, we both know it's illegal.

She exhales. I smell alcohol and morphine on her breath.

'I never ran an abortion clinic in the first place, Jack, you know that. There's no crime in handing out French letters and diaphragms, is there? I just provided contraception assistance for poor bloody women trying to avoid getting in the family way. Poor bloody women too alone, or too afraid, or too sick to have a child. Poor bloody women…like your sister.' Her eyes are gimlets. 'You raided me a few times. Was I ever doing anything illegal? No. And no woman who came to see me woman ever complained. To this day I can't understand why I was run out of town.'

'We never figured out who started the fire. Still, you survived. You'll always survive. Someone always tips you off.'

'Not me. You should be looking at Maud Percy and her mob of ratbags. They're the ones who tried to murder me.'

'That's a bit far-fetched, Floss. She's difficult, I'll grant you that, but she'd never do anything like that.'

'You know, most of the women who came to me for advice were Catholic; women kept poor and pregnant by the teachings of the Catholic Church. I don't remember the Church ever telling them that they really didn't have to have a baby every five minutes just to get to heaven.' She scratches her ear. 'How is your sister by the way?'

'She died four years ago.'

'I'm sorry to hear that. What happened?'

I look away and she doesn't press me. She probably already knows and her question's rhetorical. Just to prove her point.

'So why did you come back, Floss?' I ask. 'I mean, you know it's never going to be any different.'

'I know that,' she replies, 'but I wanted to come home to die. This is my home. I have the right to die here.'

I'm searching for a lie in her words—a play for sympathy—but all I can see is a painful truth.

'You're dying?'

'Yes. It's the reward you get for living a sinful life. No matter what anyone else thinks, the truth is that I devoted my whole life to helping women.' She stops. Quietly, she adds, 'Cancer. A few months left, at most.'

'And you're here alone?'

'An old mate is looking after me.'

I take a step back. 'Well, I never thought… I mean, we're just about the same age…'

Her face drops. 'Neither did I, neither did I.'

I look at my feet and shift my weight. 'Since I'm here anyway, would you mind if I asked you a quick question?'

She snorts, as if she's been waiting all along for the sting in my tail, and she's just felt it. 'Right,' she mutters.

'You didn't happen to help a young girl deliver a baby in the last few weeks?'

'Take a look at me, Jack,' she replies, 'do I honestly look as if I'm capable of delivering a baby? I'd be flat out delivering a letter, these days.'

I watch her hand shake and can't help but agree. It was a silly question and, even though I'd like to ask her another, I let it go. 'Look after yourself, Floss,' I say instead. 'Try to stay off the map.'

'Just keep that Papist lynch mob away from me. I want to die in peace.'

'I'll do that,' I reply. 'Everyone is entitled to peace in their final days.'

'You're a good man, Jack Furey.'

Her words hang around as I turn away. If I'd been a good man, things might have been very different for a lot of people.

Including my sister.

CHAPTER FOURTEEN

A few weeks later, I'm minding my own business at the station when I get a whiff of something and my thoughts turns to the dunny at the back of the stationhouse. I'm thinking that the bloody thing's probably overflowed again, when the front door bursts open and the stink hits me like a sledgehammer.

Harry Jacka's particularly ripe today. He pushes past me, full of methylated spirits and unwashed humanity, dodging every attempt to herd him back through the open door. His hands tremble but I don't think it's delirium tremens. He's blanched despite the grime, and wide-eyed.

'Sergeant, Sergeant,' he stammers. He's teetering on the edge of a breakdown.

'Harry? What's the matter?'

He sucks in air like Gracie's Hoover. 'A dead baby,' he begins. 'A dead baby...down at the creek. A little baby. A poor little mite. Dead.'

I shake my head to clear the fog that suddenly surrounds me. Mabelle? No, of course not. This must be another baby. 'What dead baby, Harry?'

'I was prospecting at Miners Creek when I found it,' he continues. 'Actually, my dog did. I saw him digging up something. I thought it was a dead animal but it wasn't… Poor little mite… So tiny, it was.'

'Are you sure?'

He tells me he knows the difference between a baby and a bilby.

'Do you think you could show me where you found it?' I don't relish a drive anywhere with Harry Jacka. 'If I met you out at the creek, could you take me where you found it?'

He frowns and I dread his reply. 'We'd get there a lot faster if you'd give me a lift,' he says.

'Right.' If he sits beside me, I'll have to hang my head out of the window to breathe. 'Come on then, Harry, but pardon me for saying that you need a bath. You'll have to sit in the back, all right? Just tap on the roof when we get close.'

He shrugs. 'Last time I had a bath, I got sick.'

'Let's get you outside, where I can breathe some fresh air.'

'And my dog?'

'The dog can ride up front with me.'

He leads me to the gold-crushing plant which shut down before I was born. Near it is a dam wall made of concrete, stretching right across the creek. It's holding back a fair volume of water, and it's pretty deep. The dam was fenced off a long time ago, when some bright spark realised the water was full of arsenic and lead, but the fence is falling down in places, and the council's never bothered to fix it.

I swam there as a kid with my mates. It didn't do any of us any harm.

Harry points to an old paperbark near the water's edge. 'I found the baby in a bush, back from the tree, beside a goat path.'

His dog's already under the fence and running in that direction.

'Better call him back,' I tell him.

Harry whistles and the dog returns to his side.

We creep through a gap in the wire. The paperbark's huge: it's been there forever. The locals used it as a diving platform and there are initials scratched all over it. If the place was half as poisoned as they say, that tree would be as dead as a dodo and nobody in town would have been able to have a child. Just about everyone used to swim here and just about every couple came to this spot for a kiss and cuddle.

We turn off and follow a narrow goat track for about a hundred yards, passing through the chinky apple trees. The place is thick with them. These days, the trees are nothing more than a good shelter for goats or wild pigs. They're a bloody weed: broad, shrubby and thorny, and their fruit is as sour as a lemon. I don't know what the Chinese miners ever saw in them.

The dog stops dead in front of us, nose twitching, and then he crawls into the undergrowth. Harry hangs back. He's seen a ghost. He can't speak.

'That's fine, Harry, you stay here,' I say as I crouch down to take a closer look. I call the dog back and get on all fours, crawling through the undergrowth, avoiding the snags. I've plunged into a buzz of flies and the sweet odour of human death. The smell is worse in the confined space. It's overwhelming.

I've smelled it far too many times.

The dog sniffs around but I push it away. 'Get out of here, you mongrel,' I growl, calling out, 'hold on to your dog, Harry, or I'll soften its bloody ribs.'

Behind me, Harry clutches his dog like he's a life preserver. He sits on a bare patch of dirt with his sleeve to his face. I brush away the flies from the fleshy mound and look.

The body is badly decomposed; one of the arms is missing. In this heat, it's hard to know exactly how long it's been here. It's been dragged out of a shallow grave, dug up by dogs or dingoes, I'm guessing. I'm surprised any of it is still here. The baby is small, not full term. Maybe it was born dead and premature. Maybe it was aborted and dumped here.

The sight of it brings back a memory I'd rather forget. I crawl out from under the shrub. Harry lowers his arm.

'Is it a baby?' he asks.

'Looks like it.' I stand up and dust myself off.

He's telling me about some Aborigines down by the creek, and I stop listening.

'You should go and have a talk to them,' he continues. 'Fancy having a baby here and dumping it. Bloody savages. Haven't they ever heard of hospitals? Go and have a talk to them.'

'Right, let's get you home,' I reply impatiently. 'We've got work to do here.' I glimpse the filth stiffening his trouser legs and add, 'You could do everyone a favour: take a bath and change your clothes.'

He disagrees.

'Alright then, do me a favour and do not tell anyone what you've found.'

He agrees.

I don't want the town's rumour mill working overtime.

CHAPTER FIFTEEN

After I drop off Harry, I bring Mahoney and Higgins back to Miners Creek with me to help investigate. I get Mahoney to search the bushes. Taking Higgins with me, I walk down to the Aboriginal camp, about half a mile down the creek.

They're not allowed to live in the town, so they're pretty much confined to camping along the creek bed. It's a pitiful and sorry place: forty-odd humans, squeezed into corrugated iron humpies. The only running water is the creek, and there are no toilets. A lot of the children die before their fifth birthday. Some of the women work as domestics and their men are mostly out on the stations. Others have taken hard to the drink. Because of that, the camp has more than its fair share of fights.

It's a place we never look forward to coming to. The boys and I find ourselves out here fairly regularly, whenever there's been a drunken disturbance or when we're taking one of their children away, and that makes me sad. I don't enjoy taking kids away; I don't think it's my job. The sound of children screaming for their parents is enough to break a man.

Last time the government asked me to do it, I told them that there were no kids left in the camp. And that was the honest truth; there weren't any when we got there. If the government wants to take children off their parents and place them in foster homes, then let the bloody politicians come here and do it themselves. They reckon the kids will have a better chance in life, but I reckon a child's place is with its family, no matter what. The politicians can say whatever they want, but I know why they do it: they think the Aborigines are dying out and they want the children integrated with the rest of us. I'd sooner they were up front about it. If they'd asked me, I'd have told the government to let them be, and to give these people a decent place to live.

If only they'd ask.

Yeah, it's a sad place full of broken people.

The camp is quiet when we get there. One of the camp dogs barks as we approach. There's no one about, except for three old blokes sitting around a fire drinking tea. I can smell damper cooking on the fire, but I don't see any women or kids. They've probably gone bush thinking we're here to take another child.

We walk over to the old blokes and they're doing their best to ignore us. The one called Bobby's always in charge. He's smart, informed, suspicious. I crouch down on my haunches while Higgins stands arrow-straight. A group of skinny camp dogs wander over to check us out; they aren't afraid, even though we sometimes have to shoot them dead when they wander off to hunt. *Silly buggers.*

'Something wrong, Boss?' Bobby finally asks me. He doesn't look at me. It's their way. 'Look around. No trouble here today. Pretty quiet here, Boss. Thanks for letting us know you were coming.' He grins as he swigs his tea.

'It's nothing about you blokes,' I reply. 'We found a dead baby down near the old plant. The body's too decayed to work out whose baby it is. I'm wondering if you mob know anything about it?'

He throws me a quick glance and a frown comes over his face. He doesn't answer me.

'Not one of your women's babies, is it?'

'Don't know, Boss,' he replies vaguely.

I growl, 'Come on now, Bobby, don't start acting all bloody vague with me. Is it one of your babies? If it is one of your women, we're worried that she may need medical help.'

He's as silent as the grave.

Higgins reaches down and grabs him by the collar. 'Speak up, and don't play the dumb blackfella with us. Sergeant Furey is asking you a question.'

'Back in line, Constable! Go and check the camp,' I bark, and he leaves.

'That bloke, he's pretty wild.' Bobby laughs. 'I thought he might give me a flogging.'

'Come on, Bobby, you're not in trouble, nor is anyone in the camp. I just want to know if you know anything about this dead baby.'

He looks at the other men. They just nod back, but don't reply.

'That baby isn't ours,' he says finally. 'Honest truth.'

'Are you sure, you're not having me on?' I ask. 'Because if you're giving me the run-around, I'll take you down the station and throw you in the slammer until you start talking.'

'No, no, Boss,' he splutters, 'I don't want to go to that lockup. That place gives me the willies.'

'So you're telling me the truth?'

'For sure, Boss, for sure. We never heard or saw no baby there, or we would have told you.'

'Right. And you never saw anyone with a baby down that part of the creek?'

'No, no. We don't like going down that part of the creek anyway,' he continues, 'no fish there and we don't want to see people doing… you know…having…'

I finish off his sentence. 'Fornicating.'

'Yeah, that stuff. Makes us shamed to look.'

'I see.' I stand up as Higgins returns to the campfire.

'I can't see anything, Sergeant,' he says.

'Thanks, Bobby.' I add, 'Let me know if you blokes remember anything. All right?'

'Yes, Boss. No worries, Boss.'

We walk away from the camp.

'Higgins,' I say, 'a word of advice for you: control your temper. If you don't, you'll never go any further up the ladder.'

‘I thought the Abo needed a bit of prodding,’ he replies. ‘You know how they are. Act like they don’t know anything, but of course they do. Shifty bastards.’

‘Listen here and listen well: if I want you to do something like that, I’ll ask you to. You’re to leave the questioning to me. There’s a time to go the heavies, there’s a time not to. Learning when to do what comes with experience.’

‘Yes, Sergeant Furey.’

‘And as a punishment for overstepping the mark, you can clean the police ute.’

‘I won’t do it again, Sergeant.’ He’s shamefaced.

By the time we get back, Mahoney has already wrapped the body in a towel and placed it in a small box in the back of the ute.

‘Did you find anything?’ I ask him.

‘Not a thing, Sarge.’

He’s looking green around the gills. ‘You don’t look well, Mahoney. Go and have a good chunder. You’ll be right after that.’

‘No, it’ll settle,’ he replies. ‘Not easy looking at a dead child.’

‘Better get used to it, son. This won’t be the last dead baby you’ll see.’

For all his willpower, he rushes away and vomits under a tree anyway. I shake my head. Can’t remember the last time I did that.

We drop the body off at the morgue and ask if Doc McDonald is around. Apparently, he’s away until tomorrow. I’m not upset. Even for a hard old cop like me, it would be a bit rugged to do the post mortem on the same day. I can’t say that too much rattles me these days, but the sight of that tiny, mutilated creature has shaken me up more than I’m willing to admit. What gets me, is trying to figure out what kind of woman does such a thing.

I’d sooner get home early, and see Gracie and Mikey instead.

CHAPTER SIXTEEN

Just for once, I'm having a good sleep. Right now, I'm not dreaming of anything special: not the war, not dead babies, nothing, and my soul's bought itself a welcome bit of peace.

I have good nights and bad nights. Unfortunately, the bad outweigh the good. I've heard of other Diggers with the same problems taking to the drink in a big way. It's got to some blokes so badly, that they've topped themselves just for a bit of shush and some shut-eye, the poor buggers. No one I know personally, mind, but you hear stories. It isn't easy being a veteran trying to get back to normal: you tell people how you're feeling, and they'll think you're either weak, or mad, or both. Just get over it. Best to keep mum: I haven't told Gracie what the screaming's about. Killing the enemy isn't a sin in my eyes, so there's no need to tell the priest when I go to confession either.

Soon I start dreaming. *Not again.* In the distance, I hear a roar. It could be German artillery. I thought I'd left it behind, I thought I'd escaped, but it surrounds me. It's another one of their creeping barrages.

The bastards, don't they ever take a break?

I feel it rumble like thunder. I scramble down into the bunker like a rabbit down a hole, even though I know it's not much of a shelter.

It's made of wood, you see, instead of concrete like the Huns'. It splinters under fire. A Hun shell lands on you in one of our bunkers and you're mincemeat: no one will ever find you. You'll just fertilise the soil, soak into the mud, and they'll never even find your dog tag.

The barrage creeps towards the trench. Around me the blokes are nervy but I'm a sergeant, so it's my job to settle them down as best I can.

'Get ready, lads,' I shout. 'When the barrage stops, get back on that parapet!'

The Huns will be running across no man's land like a mob of wild cattle.

'Not yet! Get down!' The words are still coming from my mouth when Tommy Taylor's helmet whistles past my ear, the back of his head explodes and I'm covered in his brain. I shrug it off, grip my rifle, and start to yell orders to the blokes.

Something shakes me.

'The bastards are coming!' I yell. 'Get ready!'

Something's shaking me again. The sun's streaming into the trench, blinding me. I open my eyes, still yelling. Gracie's shaking me. My hand's on her throat.

'Darl,' she soothes, prising open my fingers and shifting my hand away from her neck, 'it's me. The phone's ringing.'

'Phone?' I reply uneasily, 'I thought...bloody hell.'

'I know, love, it's a nightmare.'

The phone is ringing out in the hallway.

She follows my eyes. 'Yes, Jack, you better answer it. It'll be for you.'

I stumble out of bed and down the hallway.

Higgins is at the other end of the line, agitated. 'Sarge, sorry to wake you up,' he stammers.

'Couldn't it wait until tomorrow?' I ask.

He doesn't hesitate. 'No, Sarge, I'm afraid it couldn't. Joe Riley at the Riley farm has just called in. He's reported a murder.'

CHAPTER SEVENTEEN

All of the lights are on at the farmhouse, and I can hear Valmay Riley shouting at Joe, even before we stop the ute. I've never been here in an official capacity, only to buy their oranges. Best you'll ever taste.

He's out of the house and running towards us, still dressed in his pyjamas. Apart from Joe and his wife, one or two labourers live at the farm, but only when they're needed. I'm wondering if the murder might involve one of them.

'Quick!' he shouts as he opens my door.

I swing my legs out. 'House or workers' quarters?'

Higgins is already out of the ute, but doesn't move.

'No, the Pilchers' place.' Joe's tripping over himself in his eagerness to get the words out. 'Kate Pilcher ran over here for help. She said there was an intruder in her house. She said the intruder killed her husband, but she got away. We rang you first and then the ambulance.' He must have caught the confusion on my face. 'The poor bugger,' he adds, 'just got home on leave.'

I ask, 'Where is Mrs Pilcher now?'

'She's inside with Valmay.'

'Good. Keep her here.' I yell over to Higgins. 'Get in! We're going over to the Pilcher place, now. Keep your eyes peeled. There may be an intruder.' I turn to Joe. 'We'll be back soon.'

The ambulance has arrived there ahead of us. I haven't seen the Pilcher place in a long time and its appearance shocks me. Some of the weatherboards are cracked and others hang off the rotting studs by a nail. In the front, there's a smashed window and part of the verandah is missing. The garden's pretty much a dustbowl.

I remember when it was an orchard owned by the Steinbocks. It was well cared for then. They were hounded out of Wangamba during the First World War, and the house was deserted until the Pilchers picked it up for a song not too long ago. They probably had nothing left to spend on it. I would have pulled it down.

Higgins is walking around the house holding a .303 rifle in one hand and a hurricane lamp in the other.

'Anything?' I ask.

'Can't really see anything much out here in the dark,' he replies. 'There's plenty to see inside.'

The ambulance men are standing at the front door having a smoke. One of them says, 'We're just waiting for you before we take the body away. There's one for the morgue in the kitchen. Just watch where you step, there's blood everywhere: floor, walls, even the ceiling. It's like a slaughterhouse.'

I squeeze past them and Higgins follows close behind, treading carefully towards the kitchen doorway. The light's on.

'Imagine that: the Huns don't get you, but some bloke breaks into your house and does you in,' Higgins remarks. 'Unlucky bastard.'

The blood sticks to our boots; the sickly-sweet smell of it clings to everything. We'll have to wash it off before we leave. In the middle of the floor next to the table, Maurie Pilcher is lying face up with a butcher's knife sticking halfway out of his chest. His eyes are wide open. He's dressed in a Jackie Howe singlet and Y-fronts. His army dog tag's covered in blood.

'Stuck it right into his heart,' I remark as I crouch down to take a closer look. 'All I can say is, it would have been quick. He would have been dead when he hit the ground.'

Higgins bends down. 'Looks frightened to me,' he observes. 'I'd be pretty scared too if I saw it coming.'

I look again. I don't see fear. 'I reckon he's more surprised than frightened. As if his last words were, "Why are you doing this?" '

I lean over and shut his eyes. I stand up and look around. It's all a bit sad and empty. There are three old wooden chairs and a bare kitchen table; one of the chairs is splintered, a second is on its side and the third chair is standing next to the wall. There's some corned beef and a piece of cheese on a platter on the dresser. There are plates and cups in the sink. Everything else seems tidy enough, squared-up and shut away. The back door is locked.

I say to Higgins, 'No one locks their houses out here.'

'Maybe Mrs Pilcher was worried about someone breaking in,' he replies.

'Possibly.'

I make some notes about what I've seen, and encourage Higgins to do the same. He scribbles for a few frantic seconds and then he slips the notepad back into his pocket. There's more to write than that. I doubt he has the makings of a detective. With the war on, we're short-staffed. Everyone has to take on more responsibility: a police sergeant's not just a police sergeant these days, and a constable has to be more than the sum of his parts.

I sketch the location of the body, the shape of the blood pool, the stain on the wall and everything else in the room, and then I send Higgins out to get the camera. By now, there's a creeping light outside, and an early dawn seeps across the horizon. I take as many photographs as I can, and then I let the ambulance officers take Maurie away.

Back at the Riley farm, we leave our hosed-down shoes to dry by the back door, and step into the kitchen in our socks. Valmay's brewing up a pot of tea.

'Now that's a welcome sight,' I say to her. 'A nice cuppa'll hit the spot.'

She smiles and pours me one.

'So,' I continue, splashing in some milk out of a bottle, 'did Kate Pilcher speak to you? When she got here?'

She replies, 'Oh, she was pretty stirred up, knocking on the door.

I'd gone to bed early, so Joe answered. She said something like, *help me, he's stabbed him…* I wasn't sure if she said her husband was dead. I can't remember exactly: I was all in a tizz, you see. Horrible what's happened.'

'Did she say who stabbed him?'

'I don't remember.'

'No matter, we'll work that one out. Could you pour me a second cup of tea please, Mrs Riley?' I ask. 'For Kate Pilcher?'

She hands me another cup, and I take both into the lounge room. I don't know a lot about the Pilchers, except that they're a young couple who moved from down south, so Maurie could work at the railways. He joined up a year ago. Last I heard, he was posted overseas. Kate is huddled on a settee with a blanket around her knees. She's pale as a sheet and her hands tremble. She still has blood in her hair and her cheek's swollen. Her eyes flit about, as if she's searching for something, yet finding nothing. I've seen other people do that before: she's in a bad state, the poor girl. I sit next to her and pass her her tea.

'Kate, can you tell me what happened?'

She looks at the tea and puts it down, stretching out her legs. She bends over, unlaces her shoes and slips them off. 'I need a smoke,' she says.

Joe Riley reaches into his top shirt pocket and hands her a packet of Woodbines. He's already smoked most of the cigarettes, so the empty part of the packet's crumpled, and the filter of the next cigarette pokes out through a hole in the top. She fumbles for it but she just can't seem to pull it out. He takes the packet from her hand and slips the cigarette between her lips. Then he lights it for her with a match.

She takes a few drags and settles. 'We had just gone to bed when I heard a window opening,' she begins. There's a sob in her voice. 'Maurie got up to see what was going on and…' She places her cigarette on the ashtray, takes out a handkerchief and presses it to her eyes. 'Some…someone…'

'Yes, Kate?'

'I came in just as he stabbed Maurie!' She begins to howl. 'He stabbed him just like that! A blackfella. I saw his face. He must've took a knife out of the drawer.'

'Did he say anything? The intruder, I mean.'

'No, I don't think so.'

'Did you recognise him? Can you tell me his name?'

'No, no. There's been a lot of blackfellas hanging around here.' She folds up her hankie and sips her tea. 'They've been hanging around like a bad smell. Stealing stuff out of the shed, peeping in the windows. Been worse since Maurie joined up.'

Joe's nodding. 'They steal oranges off us.'

'Who?'

'Those blacks at the camp.'

'It was one of the young blokes,' she cries. 'He must have come in through the kitchen window. There was a fight; I heard it, and I come into the kitchen. Then the black so-and-so put one of the butcher's knives in my poor husband's chest! My poor, dear husband! Goes through the war only to be murdered in his own home!' She screams, lets the cup drop from her hand and collapses on the floor.

Joe and I help her back up.

'Tell me you'll get him,' she pleads. 'Justice for my poor Maurie!'

I pull out my pencil and thumb through the pad to a blank page. 'Can you identify him?'

'Yes, about twenty, solid, not too tall. He has a…scar on his face.' She lifts her hand. 'About here. You asked me if I know his name. Why would I know his name? I seen him around town though. I…I…tried to fight off the blackfella when he was attacking Maurie. The bloke hit me and then he pushed me to the ground. For a moment, I thought he'd do me in also or…you know…rape me. Then he ran off.'

'That's enough for the moment. I'll ask you to come down to the station later.'

'All right,' she replies. 'I want the so-and-so caught and hung.'

'Of course you do.' Back in the kitchen, Higgins has finished his tea. 'Have a think about this.' I show him my notes. 'Anyone you know?'

He shakes his head. 'Not straightaway.' He sighs. 'It's going to be a long night, hey Sergeant?' He's weary and it shows in his eyes.

'Afraid so. There'll be plenty of time for sleep when this is done and dusted. Get Mahoney out of bed. We need everyone on duty.'

CHAPTER EIGHTEEN

So the long night ends, without any of us getting another wink of sleep. Kate Pilcher arrives at the station for her statement in the early morning, saying that she couldn't sleep and gleaming like a polished penny. I guess everyone reacts to grief differently. It couldn't have been easy to watch a loved one die like that.

I call Mahoney into the room, so he can learn how these things run. He's writing everything down too, and we'll compare notes later.

She coaxes the wrinkles out of her stockings and sits with her legs crossed. She seems careful, distant, frowning as she answers every question.

She begins, 'When Maurie first went out to see what was going on, he found the Abo going through the pantry. He'd got in through the window; he must have been looking for food. Or grog, maybe. Maurie had a carton of beer in the pantry.

'Well, anyway, Maurie closed the window and he locked the door, you know, to keep him in. Maurie was yelling: he was really angry. He said, it wasn't on, having blackfellas breaking into his house to steal stuff. I remember him telling the bloke he was going to give him the hiding of his life. He said then he'd get some mates to burn their camp down. Maurie hates...I mean hated... blacks.

He always told this story that his grandfather was murdered by one in the old days.'

'Did the intruder say anything?'

'I dunno. He tried to get out, but then Maurie started beating him. He fought back. He looked like he could box. I've seen the boxers at the show; he was as good as any of them. Maurie could fight too, but this bloke started getting on top of him. Then Maurie got the butcher's knife out of the drawer and said he was going to kill the bloke. The Abo looked scared and he tried to get out through the door, but he couldn't open it. Maurie went for him with the knife but he missed. Then he grabbed it off Maurie and stabbed him in the chest. I tried to fight the Abo off but he just threw me to the floor. I really thought I'd be next, but he just looked at me and ran for the door.'

'How did the intruder get out of the house if Maurie had locked the door?' I asked.

'I don't know. He was able to grab the key off Maurie, I suppose, and then he made a run for it. I wasn't going to stop him. I was trying to stop Maurie from bleeding to death,' she replied.

'Where did the intruder leave the key? Did he drop it or keep it?'

'How the heck would I know? I wasn't exactly watching what he was doing. After that, I ran straight over to the neighbour to call for help. We don't have a telephone, see.'

'Did you know Maurie was coming home on leave?' I ask.

'No…I suppose he wanted to surprise me.' She dabs her eyes. 'He only got home that day, you know.'

'Okay,' I tell her, 'we'll leave it at that for now. We're going to have to search your place.'

'Well, I won't be going back for a while. The Rileys said I can stay with them until all of this is sorted out.'

'And don't leave town anytime soon. I may have to ask you more questions.'

'What? Why? I've told you who it was. All you have to do is arrest him, take him to court, and hang the black so-and-so,' she snaps. 'If it was up to me, I wouldn't waste time with a bleeding trial.'

'I understand how you must feel, Mrs Pilcher, but there's a procedure we have to follow.'

'I told you everything I seen,' she cries. 'Can't you just leave a poor woman grieve for her husband in peace?'

'Well, I may need you here to identify the intruder.'

She grunts. Her hands fly up to her eyes again. She takes out a compact, powders her face and reapplies her lipstick. She notices that I'm watching her.

'Don't you judge me,' she says. 'You don't have that right. I don't want anyone pointing at me and feeling sorry for me, when they see me go past. Even if my heart is breaking inside, I'm not showing it on my face. I'm not playing the part of the widow, just to keep you happy.'

I say nothing. I wind up the interview and head out to the Aboriginal camp with the boys. It's still early. We might catch them while they're still asleep.

The mongrel dogs hear us first as we come up the creek. We're all armed with .303 rifles: we're not taking any risks with this bloke. I send Mahoney and Higgins to the outer extremities of the camp. It's a pathetic attempt to surround them but, with only three men, it's the best we can do.

Higgins kicks one of the dogs as it goes for his heel, and it falls away yelping. It's enough to wake up the whole camp. The Aborigines float out of their humpies, bewildered. Some of the kids are crying and they hide their faces in their mothers' bosoms. Mahoney and Higgins close in, rifles aimed.

Bobby comes to me with his hands up. 'Don't shoot, Boss,' he begs, 'this isn't the old days anymore, Boss. We're mates now.'

'We're looking for a man, Bobby,' I say as I lower my rifle.

Meanwhile, Higgins searches the humpies while Mahoney herds the men into a group. There are about ten of them, of varying ages.

'A white bloke was murdered last night,' I continue, as I walk up to the men, 'Maurie Pilcher.' Bobby follows me. 'A witness said it was an Aboriginal man who did it. The witness says Maurie Pilcher was murdered by one of your mob. He was murdered in front of his wife.'

'None of us. Swear, Boss.'

Bobby tries to grab my arm. I shrug him off and hold him away from me, as Higgins puts his rifle to Bobby's head.

Bobby continues, 'None of us killed no whitefella. We don't fight whitefellas no more. We mates now.' He reaches out to shake my hand but I draw back.

'You're bullshitting me, Bobby,' I growl as I grab him by the shirt collar, 'and I'm not in the mood for bullshit.'

'Swear on the Bible, Sergeant.'

I check the rest of the men over. They have their heads down. Only two of them match the age.

'Stop skulking. Put your heads up,' I order, 'and give us a good look at you.' I go from man to man, lifting their chins and checking them over. I turn to Bobby. 'Be honest with me, Bobby. If you bullshit me, I'll have you in the slammer as an accessory to this murder, all right?'

'I'm telling the truth,' he cries, lifting his hands in prayer. 'I don't want to be in that gaol.'

'Which one of your young bucks has a scar on his face? Maybe he's also done some boxing?'

He thinks for a while.

'Come on, Bobby, I've haven't got all bloody day. Give me a name or I'll take you in.'

'Yes, Boss, no worries,' he finally says. 'It sounds like Jimmy Crowbar, but he's not here. He's working on the Cunningham place, you know, Carrington Station.'

'Are you sure?' Carrington Station is about ten miles away.

'He works out there, honest truth. Been there for months now.'

'It's not impossible, Sergeant,' Higgins whispers. 'These bastards can run fast. Maybe he's smart enough to drive.'

I stare Bobby down. 'Right, I'll let you go for now, but I may be back. If I suspect you're lying to me, I'll bloody take you in.'

'No worries, Boss, honest truth. Only I don't know if Jimmy could kill anyone. He's a good man, works hard, good horseman. Christian man, you know?'

'I'm sure every murderer's a good man until he decides to murder someone,' I reply.

'Jimmy wouldn't murder anyone. No way,' he adds.

I ignore him, and signal Higgins and Mahoney that we're leaving. 'All right constables, you're heading out to Carrington Station to have a serious chat to Jimmy Crowbar. Just remember, he may be armed and dangerous, so have your rifles ready. If he resists, don't muck around with him.'

'Are you coming, Sergeant Furey?' Higgins asks.

'No, I'm going to find Doc McDonald. He needs to do two urgent post mortems.'

He sniggers and I know what he's thinking. 'Let's hope you've caught him on a good day,' he says.

CHAPTER NINETEEN

The nurses at the hospital don't know where Doc McDonald is, but I know exactly where to look. I find him at Molly Pryor's place. She's his receptionist, but she also doubles as his companion.

You see, when the Doc isn't drinking himself into a stupor, he likes to entertain himself with female company. No self-respecting woman would have anything to do with him, except that he comes from a wealthy family. I've heard he has a wife down south, but he gets around, as they say. Apparently, a few quid in the bank improves anyone's looks and character.

Just ask Molly.

There's a saying among the locals: Doc McDonald's not a bad doctor when he's sober. The last doctor, Doc Havelock, left a few years ago under a cloud, and we were stuck with McDonald. I heard McDonald was about to be deregistered because of his drinking problem when the Wangamba Hospital threw him a lifeline. Doctors aren't easy to get out here. It was Wangamba or nothing for the Doc. A drunk doctor is better than none at all, I reckon.

The Doc isn't too happy to see me; he doesn't want to do any post mortems today. I remind him that the next time I catch him driving his black Packard whilst under the influence, I won't be running him home, I'll be running him in. Funny how he changes his mind pretty quickly.

No one likes attending post mortems. You'd have to be a sick sort of bastard to enjoy it. The morgue is small and stifling: it should be cooler, but you get what you're given out here in the bush. In the big cities, it would be different. Townies don't care a hoot about our facilities. And Doc McDonald doesn't make post mortems any better. He's a law unto himself.

The stone dissection table is in the middle of the morgue. The Doc wants to do the baby first. I pull it out of the icebox and place it on the table. It's swamped by the vast flatness of the table: a tiny lump with a sheet over it. I say a prayer for the poor little bugger. I tell myself—as I always do—it's just a body being dissected, a bit of flesh, that's all. The soul is long gone.

The smell is stronger in a confined space. I'm having a bit of trouble with the odour today, but not the Doc. He isn't daunted. Maybe all of the grog he's drunk over the years has killed off his ability to smell. He pulls a bottle of whisky and a glass out of his doctor's bag. His hands are shaking, but he still manages to fill the glass to the brim. He asks if I want one. He smiles when I shake my head, and tosses it back in one gulp.

The morgue doesn't quite have the atmosphere I want when I'm having a drink.

The Doc's shakes have settled. He slips on a pair of gloves and pulls his medical instruments out of his bag. The Doc is ready.

'I'm glad you're in attendance, Sergeant Furey,' he says.

'Why's that, Doc?' I reply.

'Mahoney, that junior constable of yours that you sent here a while back to observe the PM of the foundling baby,' he continues, 'decided to become extremely unwell, but couldn't quite manage get himself outside first. Most unpleasant.'

He laughs, but I don't. We don't share a sense of humour.

'All right.' He peels back the sheet slowly and peers at the body. He prods it with his finger, turning it over once, twice. He cuts open the ribs with a pair of scissors and pulls them apart. He takes a deep breath. 'The body is in an advanced level of decomposition.

The body is…' He produces a tape measure. 'Eleven inches long. That means it was *in utero* for around five months.'

I thought as much.

'It's too badly decomposed to determine what sex it is. Possibly male, but that's only my assumption.'

'What about its race?'

'Again, can't tell.'

I'm suspecting we're not really getting anywhere with this.

'How about the cause of death?'

'Once again, difficult to tell. No indentations on the skull. There are two possibilities: a spontaneous miscarriage or an abortion, either by a backyard abortionist or by the mother herself. If the body was better preserved, I'd be able to determine if it was done by the mother.'

'How?'

'The baby's neck would have multiple abrasions due to the mother extracting it from her womb.'

'I see.' I sigh with disappointment. 'Not a very clear outcome.'

'Yes, an indeterminate result,' he replies as he drops his instruments, 'but if the mother comes to me, I'll know straight away if she's recently been pregnant.'

'Which may never happen,' I reply.

'You never know. Although, if she had developed an infection, she would have presented at the hospital by now.'

'So it might be a backyard abortionist,' I suggest, 'one that's skilled in their work?'

'Possibly. That's up to you to find out, Sergeant Furey,' he replies. He chuckles and removes his gloves while I cover the body and return it to the icebox.

The Doc pours himself another whisky.

'You know you've got another one,' I say.

'Of course I do. I'm feeling a little peckish,' he says. 'When you're ready, can you go to the hospital kitchen and get me some morning tea? Get something for yourself, too.'

I shake my head. The Doc gave up his humanity long ago. I wonder if the transition happened when he was training to become a doctor. I suppose it's possible that he was always the same. I'm searching for a glimpse of his soul, but it's as absent as the corpse's. Maybe he's just as human as the rest of us, and it's just the grog that helps him cope.

I head off to the kitchen and get back ten minutes later. The Doc has done me a good turn by getting Maurie Pilcher out of the fridge and putting him on the table.

'Good,' he says, 'I'm ravenous.' He bites into a sandwich.

I begin, 'This man was stabbed in the chest when he was at home, in his kitchen. He was on leave from the army.'

'Tsk,' he says. 'Don't tell me another thing. I don't want any preconceptions, you see. It may blind me to the obvious, and cloud my mind.'

And the whisky's not already doing that?

'Right,' I say and keep quiet.

'I've taken a look at him while you were off getting our morning tea. I don't know if you noticed this too, but part of his right ear is missing. It's an old cut, clean, done by something very sharp, possibly a razor.'

'So, not done at the time of the murder.'

'Oh no, it's well healed. Done years ago.' He continues, 'He has some recent superficial cuts and bruising to his hands and to the back of the skull, and the latter's probably as a result of falling backwards and striking the floor. Aside from that and the wound to the chest, there's not a fresh scratch on the rest of him.' The Doc bends over and stares at the chest wound. 'See,' he says, pointing with the crust of his sandwich at a gaping wound where the ribs meet the breastbone, 'this was done by a large knife. Sharp, it was. No ripping of the flesh.' He finishes chewing and measures the cut. Then he gloves up and picks up a scalpel. 'Nicked the costal cartilage on the way through. Under and up. Probably would have sliced his heart right open, like a piece of fruit. Certainly didn't do it to himself. The perpetrator didn't try to pull the knife out.' He makes some notes. 'Can't remember the last time we had a murdered cadaver in here, actually. Can you, Sergeant?'

It's been a while. 'So, he died instantly?'

'I can't say yet that that was definitely what killed him, but if you're asking me if he knew what was happening, even with a cut to the heart, it can take a little while to lose consciousness. He'd certainly have known about it.' He shakes his head. 'It's a shame the dead can't talk and the best they've got is us. It makes you wonder, what's happening to the place?'

'Well, it was obviously the butcher's knife to the heart that killed him,' I continue, 'that should be enough for the autopsy report, shouldn't it? I mean, it's obvious he died from the stab wound. You can sign off on that now, can't you?' At this point, I'm hoping Doc McDonald is eager to return to Molly's warm embrace. I'm hoping that accepting my suggested cause of death will be as advantageous for the Doc as it is for me. One thing I don't really like watching is when he has to cut open the skull and pull the brain out. Brains remind me a bit too much of scrambled egg.

Since the Great War ended, I've never eaten scrambled eggs.

The Doc picks up his saw. 'No, I'll have to give this poor chap the full beauty treatment.'

'All right,' I reply quietly and retreat to the corner of the room. 'I guess you have to do it all properly.'

'Help yourself to a sandwich,' he offers, 'there's plenty there.'

I shudder as he starts to saw into the skull. 'No thanks.'

An hour later and it's done, thankfully. He concludes that the stab wound was indeed the cause of death. Maurie Pilcher's a sorry sight, but I keep telling myself that his soul is elsewhere, and that's the best thing I can say about that. The Doc finishes up by putting Maurie's brains into his gut cavity, and then roughly stitching him up. He tells me he can't put the brains back into the skull cavity as they've expanded too much.

He takes off his gloves and gown, scrubs his hands and returns to what's left of his morning tea.

If their loved ones only knew.

CHAPTER TWENTY

Maud Percy's back. God, give me strength.

'Sergeant Furey,' she barks even before she gets to the front counter, 'we need to speak.'

The boys are still away, but they're due back soon. Not soon enough, sadly, for me to peddle her off to one of them. Right now, I'm the only one at the station.

'What's it about this time?' I reply, rolling my eyes.

'Well,' she exclaims, 'you don't have to be so flippant, Sergeant Furey! Show some respect!'

'Now, now, don't get yourself all in a dither.' I patronise her. 'Getting yourself all worked up won't help you.'

She sucks in her lips until they're two thin strokes of red. It's as if she's underlined her nose twice. 'I heard you've found a dead baby at the creek.'

'Is that so? Well, I'm not confirming or denying that. I'm not free to discuss police matters with a member of the public,' I reply.

'I'm not just a member of the public,' she goes on, 'I'm a member of the Catholic Church. When children are aborted and dumped like rubbish, I need to know.'

'You see, Mrs Percy, I don't think you do.'

She grunts. 'Miss Percy, Sergeant Furey. Why must you insist…'

'Why must you?' I interrupt.

'...on getting it wrong,' she continues.

I take in a breath. 'And you're here because?'

'You must do something about that horrible Floss McCarthy. No doubt you haven't even bothered to visit her since I was last here, and you clearly haven't warned her out of town.'

'I have visited her but, no, I didn't warn her out of town. I've told you, she has the right to live wherever she wants to,' I reply curtly.

'But that is unacceptable, Sergeant Furey!' she barks. 'You must arrest her for killing that child. It's obvious she killed that child. Who else would have done it?'

'Between, you, me and the fencepost, Miss Percy, if there was a baby—and I'm not saying there was—it is a matter for the police, and only the police. It's not a matter for do-gooders and busybodies. I'll say it once again: leave Floss McCarthy alone. Leave her alone,' I repeat as calmly as I can. 'Now, I have work to do. Get out.'

For a while, she doesn't speak. The old biddy is, for once in her life, lost for words. It's a pity that it's not a permanent arrangement. She stands there, gulping air like a beached guppy.

'There will be consequences out of this, mark my words, Sergeant Furey,' she finally shrieks. 'Father Donnelly will be most concerned to hear of your actions. Most concerned.' She spins on her heel and storms out.

I take a deep breath and can only imagine the grief I'll get over this. I don't really want to get in his bad books.

No sooner has Maud Percy left, than Mahoney and Higgins drag in Jimmy Crowbar.

'So, Constables, did he give you any trouble?' I ask as they walk him towards the counter. Crowbar fits the description that Kate Pilcher gave me, though I don't see much of a scar on his face. You'd have to look pretty closely to see it.

'We had a bit of trouble. The boong resisted, so we had to manhandle him a bit,' Higgins says.

There's crusted blood around Crowbar's nose, and one of his eyes is bloodshot. There are scabs across his knuckles and the back of his hands. He speaks to me, his head lowered, 'I dunno why I'm here. They asked what I was doing yesterday, and I told them.'

'Shut it,' Higgins growls as he shoves Crowbar against the counter. 'You're a murderer; you were seen. It doesn't come better than that. You've got a one-way trip to the lockup, blackfella.'

Crowbar's mouth drops open. 'But I never murdered nobody! I'm a good Christian. Honest!' His eyes whip around the room, big as dinner plates. 'You blokes got the wrong blackfella. Ask Mr Cunningham, Sarge.'

'Every criminal we've ever arrested says he's innocent, but we know you aren't.' Higgins shoves him again.

'All right, settle down,' I snarl. 'Back in line, Higgins!' He looks at me like a reprimanded dog and backs away. I lift up the flap at the end of the counter and Mahoney leads Crowbar towards the cell. 'Jimmy Crowbar, you've been brought here in connection with the murder of Maurice Pilcher. Do you understand?'

'What?' Crowbar shouts and jostles against Mahoney in a frenzied attempt to return to the counter. 'I swear, I don't know no such bloke. I never left Carrington Station for weeks, like I said. Mr Cunningham will tell you where I was. You ask him yourself.'

'You're not talking bulldust are you, Crowbar?'

'No bulldust. Or bullshit, neither,' he replies.

'All right, then, I'll ask him. I'll give him a call.' I return to the counter and pick up the handset, and begin to ask the telephonist to connect me.

'That would be good, Sarge,' interrupts Higgins, 'except that he's away at the moment on a muster. The housekeeper doesn't know a thing, and she didn't seem to know when he'll be back. Convenient, hey?'

I put down the telephone and shake my head. 'Well, we can't just let you go, Jimmy. You're going to have to stay here at least until we either exclude you as a suspect, or Bill Cunningham returns, whenever that is. And if you're lying to me…'

Crowbar whimpers as Mahoney opens the cell door, urges him through and then locks it behind him. He looks around and sits on the bare bed, his head in his hands. 'But I done nothing wrong. Honest.'

The best I can say is, 'We'll see.'

I send Higgins and Mahoney home for some shut-eye. I can't lock up the station now that Crowbar's in the cell, and I tell Mahoney he can have the night off, but Higgins will have to return for the overnight shift. He's none too pleased, I can tell you.

Late in the evening, we bring Kate Pilcher in to identify Jimmy Crowbar, and she looks as if she's seen a ghost. 'I think that's him,' she says at first, and then she falls back into Higgins's arms.

I eye her suspiciously. 'You *think* that's him? You're not sure?' I ask.

'Oh yes, it's him alright. Yes, that's the blackfella that killed my husband. I'd recognise him anywhere.'

By the time she signs a statement to that effect, it's nearing midnight and it's been a very long time since I was last in bed. I leave Higgins in charge and go home for a few hours.

'Ring me if he gives you any grief, or if you need anything,' I tell him. 'I'll be back again in the morning.'

What greets me in the morning is nothing short of a bloody shemozzle.

I look at Higgins but he turns away, and Mahoney's face is as blank as his intellect. 'What in God's name did you do to him?'

Jimmy Crowbar's curled up on the bed, nursing his ribs and his face has blown up like a balloon. I glare at Higgins. Eventually, he meets my eye.

'He was playing up something shocking, so I just thought I'd give him a bit of a touch-up, you know, to quieten him down a bit.'

'But didn't I tell you that if he gave you any trouble to ring me? So, why didn't you ring me?'

'You seemed pretty tired, Sarge, and I had things under control...'

'You had things under control? You call this, having things under control?'

Jimmy Crowbar groans. At least he's not dead.

'Look, he's the criminal here, not me,' he replies. 'He's a cold-blooded murderer and a boong. So what if he's got a black eye?'

'We don't have lynch mobs here. A judge will decide Crowbar's guilt or innocence, not you.' I take Higgins aside so that Mahoney can't hear, and put my face so close to his that we breathe the same air. 'I've just about had enough of your insubordination, Constable, and if I had any choice in the matter, I'd have you out of here so fast that your head would still be spinning on your fiftieth birthday. This damn war means that you have to stay put for the time being. But the war won't last forever. Let me make one thing clear to you: I'm in charge, not you. I can make your career pleasant or unpleasant, and right now you're making it a really easy choice for me. One more incident and, war or no war, you'll be up on a charge. Do you understand me?'

'But Sarge…'

'You'll address me from now on at all times as Sergeant Furey. Do you understand me?' I bellow.

'Yes, Sergeant Furey,' he replies.

'Good. You will never touch anyone again, except under my express order. Do you understand me?'

'Yes, Sergeant Furey.'

'Right. Now get Dr McDonald over here quick-smart, and have him take a look at Crowbar. You're staying put until he's given the all-clear. Then you'd better go home, get some sleep and recover your bloody senses, Constable.'

'Yes, Sergeant Furey.'

CHAPTER TWENTY-ONE

A couple of days later I hear from the fingerprint bureau, but the news is just as frustrating as the rest of the investigation's been so far. The handle of the knife was wiped clean and there were no prints detected on the weapon, and that's both bad and good news for Jimmy Crowbar.

It's bad news, because he can't be excluded. It's good news, because I don't think he'd have gone to the trouble of wiping the handle before making his dash for freedom through a door he's had to unlock with a key. I have to say I was always a little sceptical, and that simply adds to it.

So, where am I now? Mahoney and Higgins have proved themselves a bona fide liability. I have two lives that ended before they began, and not a clue where to start looking for their mothers. I have a bloke still cooling his heels in the morgue, because his wife can't afford to bury him. I've got a bloke in my lock-up who matched the wife's description and whom she's now identified, but who swears his boss can give him an alibi. Which would be fine, except that his boss just happens to be in the middle of nowhere, and we can't ask him. I've got the wife with no obvious reason to kill her husband, who spins me a yarn with holes so big, I could drive a Matilda tank through them.

I ask myself, is there something else behind all of this? I'm thinking that maybe it's time to take another look. I pencil in another trip to the Pilcher house, and settle down to catch up on my paperwork. As ever, it's the minute I get stuck in that someone will come through the door and require my attention.

And today is no different.

'Well, well, Miss Percy,' I say, 'you're back. What is it now?'

Her lips are as tight as a drum. She looks about, as if she's expecting to be overheard, and then leans in. 'I believe there may be a bawdy house operating in King Street,' she begins in a low voice. She looks around again, and stands up straight as an arrow. 'Now, I'm sure you can't turn a blind eye to that, Sergeant.'

I desperately want to roll my eyes. 'What makes you think that there's a brothel there?'

'Well, I heard from one of the neighbours that she's seen comings-and-goings all time of the day and night. Although, mostly the night. And nearly all of them are men.'

'So why hasn't she come here to tell me this herself?'

'She's frightened of being seen walking into the station. She's worried about the consequences. I, on the other hand, being a long-time campaigner for morality and fairness, hold no such fear.'

'No. You're here every few days.'

Lucky me.

'So,' she continues, 'you will go there and shut it down.' It's a statement, not a question.

I reply, 'I will use my experience and knowledge to do whatever I believe I should do, to make sure the law is upheld.'

She grunts. 'As uncooperative as ever, I see, Sergeant. You know Father Donnelly had a word about you to Mrs Furey.'

Now, she's got my goat. 'What! What about?'

'We're all worried about your moral decline. Ever since that woman returned, you're a changed man.'

'What are you insinuating?'

'Nothing, Sergeant. I'm insinuating nothing. But we both know there's a family history…'

I'm flabbergasted. I've never wanted harm to befall a person quite so much since I left the army. 'You, Miss Percy, are a busybody and a hypocrite. I urge you to take a look at yourself before you look at others. I'm certain you know the gospel: you're always reading the Bible during Mass. I'm referring to the bit about removing the log out of your own eye first.'

'Well!' she replies. 'Father Donnelly…'

'What a good idea,' I continue. 'Perhaps you should both read Matthew, chapter seven, verse five, before either of you talks to my wife about me and my morals again.' I turn away. 'Good day, Miss Percy, I happen to be very busy at the moment, making sure that we're all safe to walk the streets without anyone bothering us.'

She's out of the door before I return to my desk, although I fear she'll be back before too long.

In the early afternoon, the front door flies open and there's Bill Cunningham. He's a big bloke, but worse than that, he's livid. He marches across the room, vaults the counter and shoves Mahoney out of the way.

'You stupid copper bastards,' he growls, 'you better release my boy right this minute, or there'll be hell to pay.'

Higgins lunges at him. 'You've assaulted a policeman!'

Cunningham shoulders him aside and rattles the cell door. Crowbar looks up. 'What in God's name… What have you done to him?' In the blink of an eye, he's taken the key off the hook and unlocked the door. He takes hold of Crowbar's forearm. 'Come on, Jimmy. You're going home with me.'

Mahoney's nipping at his heels. I can see bad descending into worse. I insert myself between Cunningham and the constable. 'A bit of calm here, a bit of calm,' I bellow. 'Now hold on for a moment, Mr Cunningham…'

'You've got the wrong man, Sergeant Furey,' Cunningham continues. 'My housekeeper filled me in. She said she told your bloody constables that we were shooting dingoes when this murder happened. That's the absolute, bloody truth. She reckons she even showed them the three bloody dead dingoes and the rifles still in the ute, just to prove it. I've even brought them down with me, to show you. I figure, you might have a few more smarts than your constables.'

I sense Cunningham's not lying.

Crowbar's doubled over: the Doc confirmed his ribs are cracked. 'That's what I told them,' he says breathily, 'but who believes a blackfella? No one.' He tells me how he shot one of the dingoes, the one with three white socks, clean through the left flank with his .22. 'Go take a look,' he says.

I reply, 'There's the issue of the identification by the victim's wife.'

'Really?' says Cunningham, 'Well, she's lying. I will swear on a stack of bibles that Jimmy and I were together the whole day and night. He hasn't left the station in weeks. Not once.'

'Right.' I frown at Mahoney and Higgins. 'Let's see those dingoes.'

They're pretty putrid by now, but there's one with three white socks and he's been shot exactly as Crowbar says. We get back inside and I say, 'A few more minutes, and then you can both go. I'll get a quick statement from you, Mr Cunningham, and get it signed off, so that there's no more trouble, right? I have no reason to keep Jimmy here after that.'

He grudgingly agrees.

Crowbar's still smarting, and I can't blame him. He straightens up a little. 'You lot don't care who you bring in,' he says. 'And as for that missus of his, all of us poor blackfellas look the same, hey?'

Less than an hour later, they've made their statements and gone, and I turn my attention to the constables. 'You didn't tell me about the dead dingoes or what the housekeeper told you,' I say. 'Why didn't you believe her?'

'Why should we believe the word of a blackfella over Mrs Pilcher, Sergeant Furey?' Higgins pipes up.

'Kate Pilcher gave me a description that might have matched Jimmy Crowbar. Did you ever think that, maybe, there's more than one bloke running around fitting that description? Or maybe, she has her bloody wires crossed? And it didn't occur to you that the housekeeper might have no reason to lie to you? I sent you out to enquire about Crowbar's whereabouts, that's all.'

‘You told us not to muck around with him, Sergeant Furey, so we didn’t.’

‘Mahoney’s only new, so I don’t expect him to get it right every time, but you’ve been around for a while, so why didn’t you believe the alibi, Higgins?’

‘Because…’ He looks sheepish.

‘Bloody hell, Higgins,’ I bark, ‘why would the Cunninghams lie? Have you got bloody sunstroke or something? They’re one of the most respected families in the district. They are the original settlers.’

‘Darned if I know.’ He shrugs his shoulders.

I hang my head and shake it. I’ve been shaking my head so much lately that I’m worried it’ll wobble permanently. ‘You’ve got to learn how to measure people up. Your job is to investigate crimes, uncover the truth, and not just arrest the first person that walks past you. Not everything is a neat package, just waiting for you to collect. You have to think: sometimes witnesses forget, sometimes they get things wrong, sometimes they lie.’

‘So, how do you tell the difference, Sergeant Furey? I mean, how do you know Mr Cunningham’s not lying to you?’ asks Mahoney.

‘Well, you weigh up motivation and reputation, and then look for corroboration. He had the bloody dingoes there, fellas.’

‘So what do we do now?’

‘We search the Pilcher property again, and then I might get Kate Pilcher in and ask her some more questions.’

‘Is Townsville going to send us a detective to help?’ Mahoney asks.

‘What do you reckon?’ I reply. ‘I’ve not long got off the blower with the inspector, and they’re tied up with stuff there. We’re on our own, I’m afraid, boys.’

CHAPTER TWENTY-TWO

When we get to the Pilcher place, I tell the constables to look for clues. 'Open your eyes and look for anything that doesn't make sense, and write it down. Then look for everything that does make sense, and write that down, too.'

The boys disappear in opposite directions and I go into the bedroom. A shabby dressing table in one corner with a wooden stool, two brushes, a comb and a scent bottle. A glass powder bowl with powder and a puff in it. A small wardrobe opposite half filled with clothes, men's and women's. A dressing gown on a hook. Slippers by the bed. The bed's made up, with a pink chenille bedspread over it. It's tidy enough until I begin to pull it apart.

I hear Higgins traipsing back along the hallway. 'Sergeant, these were hidden in the back of the kitchen cupboard, under some tea towels.' He shows me five packs of cigarettes.

Lucky Strikes. Yank smokes. I turn my attention to the bed. The sheets are thin and grubby, but other than that, there's nothing unusual about it. There are some hairs on the pillows. I collect them and store them in an envelope for later.

Mahoney returns soon after, with four packets of silk stockings in his hand. 'Found them next to the manhole in the roof space.'

'See anything else up there? I ask.

'I crawled up there for a better look, but all there was, was a dead possum.'

'Right.' Our girl might be trading on the black market. I look around and find no obvious signs of wealth. 'Keep looking.'

After I've scoured the bedroom, I return to the kitchen. The blood's still there, except it's dry and dark now. I do my best to skirt around it. The plates and cups are still in the sink; there's the start of mould growing on them. Something's chewed the now-maggoty corned beef and almost all of the cheese. Rats, most probably. Black flies coat the ceiling.

There's a bit of hair on one of the legs of the broken chair, and some on the top of the table. I put them in envelopes, too.

'Right,' I say, 'let's take a look at what's outside.'

We walk around the garden and the paddocks beyond, and I realise it's going to be hard to search. The place is totally covered in chinky apple trees, spear grass and weeds. *Bloody mongrel country.* I'd clear the lot. If they had bothered to run some cattle on the place, it would have kept them down.

And made it easier for us.

I notice a narrow path going down to Miners Creek. A pipe runs from the house to the creek, a few miles upstream from the gold-crushing mill and the Aboriginal camp.

'It's not a stock path,' Higgins comments. 'Maybe goats? Or kangaroos?'

My old man was a stockman and he learned a little about tracking off the Aborigines. When the old bastard wasn't drunk and flogging all of us, at least he managed to teach my brother and me a little bushcraft.

About the only decent thing he did, apart from dying.

'Human tracks made this, I reckon,' I reply. 'There must be a pump down here to get water up to the house. Spread out and look around. I'll stick to the path.'

The constables don't look happy about it. Higgins grizzles, 'There's spear grass everywhere, Sergeant Furey. Those little barby buggers are going to get in our clothes.'

'Right, well, that's just too bad, Constable, isn't it? I'm the sergeant and you're not. Spread out, noses to the ground,' I bark.

We move slowly towards the creek. Mahoney's picking his way carefully through the tall grass.

'Is there a problem, Constable?' I ask.

'I don't like snakes, Sergeant. And I really don't like walking through their back yard. One of them must bite us eventually.'

'Leave them alone and they'll leave you alone.' I stop for a while and put my hands on my hips. 'Can you two concentrate on finding evidence, rather than whingeing all the time?'

Higgins sniggers, and we keep going. Aside from Mahoney tripping over a dead stump, the search of the paddock is uneventful. I don't know what I expected to find.

Once we've reached the creek, I take a good look at the pump. It's rusted out and bits of it are lying in the grass. 'It hasn't worked for ages. They must have just used rain water.'

'So, why have the path?' Higgins asks. 'It's not like there's a swimming hole here, and there isn't enough water to fish out of. It's pretty bloody dry, actually.'

'Someone has been beating a path to the farm house,' I reply, 'and pretty regularly, from the look of it.'

'Sergeant,' Mahoney calls out, 'come have a look at this!'

There's something in one of the chinky apple trees near the creek bank. It's a bit of fabric caught up in a thorn. I pick it off the bush and place it in an envelope.

'What do you reckon it is?' he asks.

'Don't know yet,' I reply.

I have a thought, but I'd sooner keep it to myself right now.

CHAPTER TWENTY-THREE

I drop into the Riley farm alone. I'm expecting to find Kate Pilcher there, and I want to ask her a few questions, but Joe tells me that she's gone into town with Valmay.

He brews up a pot of tea, and we settle down for a chat. Or at least, that's what he thinks we're having.

'How's your house guest been?' I ask him.

He chuckles. 'She's a bit of a handful, I have to tell you. I dunno what's wrong with the girl: one minute she's as jumpy as a flea on a herd of cattle, the next she's fast asleep and Valmay can't rouse her. I suppose it's to be expected. It must be hard to have your old man stabbed to death right in front of your eyes.'

I nod. 'Yep, it's got to be hard.' I sip my tea. 'Has she said anything to you about what happened that night? I'm thinking that it might help the poor girl if she talked about it.'

'Not a word. You really reckon it would help her to talk about it? You ever talk about what you seen during the last war with anyone?'

'Not a soul, Joe, not a soul.'

'Well, maybe it's the same with her. Maybe she doesn't want to think about it. Maybe she's got no words left.'

'Hmm.' I think it over. 'The truth is, we haven't been able to find anyone matching the description she gave us. Thought we had someone, but it turns out he and Bill Cunningham were shooting dingo together. Bill's given him an alibi.'

'Known Bill Cunningham for over fifty years, and I've never known him to tell a lie. Honest in life and in business. He gives a bloke an alibi, and you can be sure he's telling the truth. The real bloke's probably left. He's probably long gone by now.'

'Possibly.' I stare at the horizon, following the wire fence that separates the Riley farm from the road with my eyes, travelling from post to post until a copse of gums blocks my view. 'You seen anything odd around here? Before the murder, I mean. Anyone or anything out of place?'

'Huh, funny you should ask that. I was just thinking it over myself the other day, and I meant to ring you. About a week before the murder, I seen a car drive down towards the Pilchers' place. Pretty flash. A black Buick, I think it was.'

My ears prick up. 'Did you happen to see who was in the car?'

'See him? I met him. You see, the stupid bugger got himself lost. Turned up at my doorstep, all surly-like, like he was itching for a fight. Valmay answered the door and I was right behind her. He asked for Maurie Pilcher by name.'

I take out my notepad and pencil. 'Can you describe him for me?'

Joe scratches his head. 'He was pretty average in height, maybe not as tall as most men. Well-fed. If he was a boxer, he'd be a middleweight. He had a couple of old scars on his face made me think maybe he was.'

'Did you happen to see the colour of his hair and his eyes?'

'Nup, he was wearing a flash hat and a nice suit. With stripes, I think. I was too dazzled by it to notice anything else.'

'Was there anyone with him?'

'Not that I saw.' He pauses. 'Oh wait, yes, there was. In the car. A girl. She didn't get out, so I never got a look at her. Maybe Valmay saw her. You could ask her.'

'So what happened then?'

'I told him that Maurie Pilcher was in the army, but his wife was probably around. Then I showed him where the Pilcher place was, and he left. Saw the car drive back the other way, not too long after.' He frowns. 'You reckon he could have done it?'

'Well, not unless Kate Pilcher's colour blind,' I reply. 'Or lying.'

CHAPTER TWENTY-FOUR

I drive straight back into town after I leave Joe Riley. I think I'll visit the dance hall and catch up with the Diamond Dolls, and my old mate Tommy Sharman while I'm there.

I pull up outside the Swing Time and walk up to the door, but it's locked. I'm not really surprised. It's probably still a bit early to expect anybody to be there.

As I return to my car, my thoughts turn to old Maud Percy, and it makes me cringe. King Street. I didn't write down the number, because I never take much of what she has to say particularly seriously, but I'm at a loose end right now and nothing's tying up.

You know what they say about idle hands.

Five minutes later, and I'm turning left onto King Street. Not for any specific reason, mind. You get to my age, and you start to feel things in your waters, whatever they are. Let's say, I felt it in mine.

King Street's not especially nice: it's full of two-room miner's cottages built out of corrugated iron and pretty much anything else the old miners could lay their hands on. Bare gardens, tumbledown fencing and filth: not somewhere anyone with a couple of quid would choose to call home.

I slow right down and inch past urchins playing cricket in the middle of the dirt road with sticks and rolled up rags. I think of

Mikey, and how different I expect his life will be from theirs. Most of them ignore me, barely moving out of my way, but one of them calls me a *sodding bastard*, and I shake my head at him and mark him down for a return visit some day.

A swift boot up the arse, I'm reserving for that lad. It might just save his life.

I think about Mabelle's mother and I can't understand why, in all of Wangamba, she'd pick a house in this street to abandon her baby. Perhaps she was from here. If Gracie's right and Bernadette Douglas was her mother, perhaps she chose it because it was about as far away from home as she could get.

I'm just past halfway down the street—the better end—where the cottages thin out. The blocks are larger now, and flaking timber houses sit in the middle of vine-riddled, overgrown gardens. There are no children here, just an old truck, a bicycle leaning against a fencepost, an Austin and a slick, black Buick, all huddled together like a witches' conclave in front of number ten.

I speed up past them, hoping that nobody's spotted me, and head back to the station.

'Right,' I tell two bored-looking constables. 'How'd you like to raid a brothel?'

Mahoney looks like it's Christmas morning and I've just handed him a present, and Higgins has already leapt to his feet.

'When? Now?' says Mahoney.

At any moment, I expect him to start dancing about, he's so excited.

'Right now. Shut up shop. Let's go.'

Mahoney and I are in my car, and Higgins follows us in the ute. This time, I'm entering King Street from the other end. I sigh, relieved, as soon as the Buick comes into sight. *It's still there.*

I pull up as near as I dare to one side of the Buick, and signal for Higgins to fence him in with the ute. Sharman's not going anywhere, not in his car, at least. He wants to do a runner, he'll have to do it on foot.

I send Higgins around the back, and Mahoney and I walk up the steps to a landing that's never seen a broom. I chuckle at the memory of Mrs Singleton telling me how she found Mabelle in a box when she came out to sweep it. I signal Mahoney to stay hidden behind the overgrowth, while I rap on the door.

Mrs Singleton opens the door and she gawps when she realises it's me. She's lost for words. Eventually she yells, 'Sergeant Furey!' far too loud for it to be a greeting. 'If...if this is about...'

Meanwhile, my size ten boot's in the door. I press all my weight against it, and the door flies wide open. Mrs Singleton's smacked flat against the wall of an entrance hall, which she's set up like a doctor's waiting room. Mahoney rushes past me and dives through the first door he sees, and I hear a woman scream. As I hurry past, I spot Snowy McIntyre sitting on one of the chairs. He notices me and hides his face.

Mrs Singleton's now recovered, and she's swinging a rounders bat at me. I grab it off her and push her down, and she tumbles backwards like a sack of manure. I toss the bat back out the door and into the garden, and she joins in the screaming that's coming at me from every corner of the house.

Higgins has come in through the rear and he's tearing up the back passage, just as a large, naked man escapes from one of the rooms and scurries down it. In a second, Higgins has forced him down and he straddles him. Together, they're blocking all access to the back door. Higgins knocks him out with a right hook, flips him over and handcuffs the man.

For the first time in a long while, I'm actually glad he's here.

In a matter of minutes, we've got one girl handcuffed to a bed post, and a second to a water pipe in the kitchen. Two Diggers are cooling their heels in one of the bedrooms. There's a third girl wearing nothing but a pair of drawers, handcuffed to Mahoney, and he's looking pleased as punch.

Just then, I see Tommy Sharman sitting in a closet off the hallway, watching the mayhem around him, mouth open, looking stunned. He's stripped the closet of its shelves, and it seems that he's been using it as his tiny office. Since Higgins knocked out the naked man right by the closet door, Sharman's now wedged behind the small card table where he's been counting money. He's busy stuffing ten shilling notes into his breast pocket, while the coins clatter to the floor.

With the last of the notes stuffed into his shirt, he tries to wriggle out from behind the desk, but the closet door's half shut and it's pressing up against him.

'Ah, Mr Sharman,' I say as I climb over the naked man. 'Good to see you again so soon.'

He's staring daggers at me and, while I can't hear what he's saying, I can read his lips. What's coming out of his mouth is as blue as a midsummer's sky, so I slam the closet door in his face, and secure it with its barrel lock.

CHAPTER TWENTY-FIVE

It's not until Higgins and I try to move the naked man that I realise we've hit the jackpot. I didn't recognise Mayor Jessop minus his clothes and the sneer on his face. By the time I've accounted for everyone, he's come around and he's baying for blood.

I toss Jessop his clothes, and tell Higgins to help him dress. I figure it'll serve as his punishment for exceeding orders, yet again.

'I'll have you sacked,' Jessop's yelling at me. 'I'm the mayor; I know people in high places.'

'Is that so, Your Worship? In my experience, the only thing people in high places are good for, is pissing on you from a great height.'

I telephone the Australian army base from Mrs Singleton's, and a couple of MPs arrive a few minutes later. I turn the two servicemen over to them, and notice that nobody's looking particularly worried about it. I'm not surprised: they're boys under pressure. During war, morality takes a back seat, even in Wangamba.

But not on my watch.

I leave Mahoney to stand guard with his truncheon drawn, and make especially certain that Tommy Sharman stays put until we can take him to the station. After that, Higgins and I begin the first of the two trips needed to bring everyone in: the three girls, Mayor

Jessop, Snowy McIntyre, Mrs Singleton and, of course, Tommy Sharman.

As luck would have it, I've just helped Mayor Jessop and two of the girls from the car, when I spot Maud Percy making a beeline for the station.

'Yoo hoo,' she calls out, scurrying towards us, 'Sergeant Furey.'

Mayor Jessop catches sight of her too, and he lifts his arm and tries to hide his face. Since he's handcuffed to one of the girls, all that does is open up the décolletage of the girl's dressing gown, and bares one of her shoulders. I have to commend Higgins in doing a stellar job in dressing Jessop: his shirt tails stick out of his gaping fly, and the effect is magnificent.

I glimpse old Maud's face. She's beside herself.

'Dear God in heaven!' she exclaims, crossing herself furiously as she peers at the girl first, and then at the mayor's crotch. 'Mayor Jessop?'

He drops his arm and the girl's decent again, but I fear the damage is done. He knows it too. 'Just helping Sergeant Furey bring in…' he mutters, but his face betrays him.

'Well,' I say, 'now you know that's a bloody lie.' I turn to Maud Percy. 'You were right, Miss Percy, there was a brothel operating out of King Street, just as you thought. We raided it today. Constable Higgins and I are just bringing in the occupants.'

I'm no longer worried that the mayor may use his influence to avoid the sting of the law. His fate is far worse. Maud Percy's tongue is the equivalent of death by a thousand cuts.

Once we get everyone back to the station and into the cells, Higgins starts the job of filling out charge sheets and interviewing. Everyone is singing roughly from the same hymn sheet: it's a therapeutic massage centre, the girls administer physical therapy, and there's definitely no hanky-panky.

Physical therapy. Without any clothes on. In a bed.

I call in Doc McDonald to perform examinations on the girls, and he tells me that what he's discovered is consistent with the premises being used as a knocking shop, rather than a kneading shop.

He draws me aside. 'One of the girls is pretty young. You need to know that she's given birth fairly recently. She's a bit of a mess; I'd say she delivered herself. She's got scars that are still relatively new.'

I stare into the Doc's bleary eyes. 'You mean… So, she might be one of the mothers we've been looking for.'

'I'd say almost certainly.'

Doc McDonald finishes up, and he's about to leave when Tommy Sharman starts rattling his cage and demanding that someone get him his lawyer.

'You fucking animal, Furey!' he screams. 'Look at what you done to me!'

It's true that I might have let him get the better of me, and I might have given him a bit of a touch-up. I might have also asked Mahoney to take the potholed route back to the station with him tied up in the back of the ute.

'Shut up, Sharman,' I bellow back at him. 'You'll get your go, when I'm good and ready.'

I turn to the Doc. 'You want to give him a once-over, and sign off that you found him in tip-top condition?'

He smiles. 'Never saw anyone in better health.' Then he takes a look at Tommy Sharman and starts. He leans into me. He's staring at me goggle-eyed. 'I know him!' he whispers.

'You sure?' I ask. 'He's not from around here, you know?' The Doc's not got the best reputation for clarity of recall.

He nods and takes me to one corner. 'About ten years ago, I worked at St Vincent's Hospital, down in Darlinghurst. I treated that man; I sutured his face.' He continues, 'I don't remember much about my patients usually, especially not after ten years, but he was particularly memorable because of the company he kept.'

The Doc's leapt up in my estimation. 'That makes sense. He told me he came up here from Sydney.' I swivel around to look at the scars crisscrossing one of his pudgy cheeks. 'Can you tell me anything about him?'

The Doc's earnest now. 'You heard of Tilly Devine?' he asks.

'The razor gang wars? Of course. Hasn't everyone?'

'Well, this man ran with her mob. When I met him, he was a pimp, a distributor of illicit cocaine and a thug. He'd found himself on the wrong side of someone wielding a cutthroat razor. I doubt very much he's changed.'

'Right.' I remember something the Doc mentioned during the autopsy. 'Maurie Pilcher. You said that the top of one of his ears had been cut off. You said it was a clean cut. Do you think…?'

'…that it was cut off with a razor?' He finishes my sentence.

'Well?' I urge.

He smiles. 'Very likely. And not a coincidence, either. I shouldn't be the least surprised if Mr Pilcher and Mr Sharman were very well acquainted before either of them set foot in Wangamba.'

'That's what I'm thinking too,' I reply.

CHAPTER TWENTY-SIX

After an hour, I let Snowy McIntyre go. He swears he had no idea of the true nature of the business being transacted back at Mrs Singleton's, and I doubt that I could prove he did. And just as well. He'd have probably lost his job, and he would have had the devil of a time explaining it to his mother.

A few minutes later, Higgins finishes interviewing Mayor Jessop, and I agree not to take matters further, provided he immediately retires from council and never seeks public office again. Truth is, I'd never be allowed to charge him. The powers-that-be protect people like Jessop, and I've already been told that my strict moral code has no place in wartime Queensland.

Lighten up, Jack!

Two of the girls turn out to be seasoned pros, and Mrs Singleton has prior convictions for soliciting and pandering in Townsville. They'll have the book thrown at them; the women always do. The third girl, the one Doc McDonald identified as recently having had a baby, sits in the lock-up apart from the others. Tears run down her cheeks like dripping taps, but she doesn't sob.

I ask Mahoney to bring her to me for questioning. She sits opposite me saying nothing, her eyes lowered, slowly wringing her hands.

'Bernadette?' I say softly, and she looks up.

'How…' she begins. 'How do you know my name? I cut my hair and told everyone my name was Lily.'

'You're Minnie and Bert Douglas's girl aren't you? You attend Mass at the Holy Family most Sundays?' It's not that I recognise her. I don't study the youngsters attending Mass that closely.

She's frightened now. 'You know them? Oh, please don't tell them! Please don't tell my parents. Please… I beg you!'

I sigh. 'You're in a heap of trouble, Bernadette; you know that, don't you? And it's not just about the kind of work you've been doing…'

'I didn't have a choice,' she begins, 'I had no money and nowhere else to go…'

I grit my teeth. 'It's also about the fact that you abandoned your baby.'

She stares at me with eyes like the sea on a stormy day and, for a while, she's struck dumb. She opens her mouth, but the sound she makes is so pained, it cuts straight into my heart.

'Dear Lord!' She doubles over and rocks. 'They told you about that? They said I had to give her up. They said she'd go to a good home. They said she'd be all right.'

'Who said that? Mrs Singleton?'

She nods. 'And the other girls.' After a while, she adds, 'I don't know how I ended up like this.' She wipes her face on the sleeve of her dress.

I hand her my fresh handkerchief and tell her she can keep it. She says she doesn't have one, and she's touched by the gesture.

'I didn't know much about where babies come from,' she says. 'Mum never said a word to me about those things. Well, of course I knew that women had babies in their bellies, and I've seen animals doing things, but I suppose I never really put the two together.'

'Well, you must have known something. The only immaculate conception I've ever heard of involved Our Lady. And your baby must have had a father.'

'Well, yes…'

'Surely, he could have done the right thing by you. You're not eighteen yet, are you?'

She shakes her head. 'I'm sixteen.'

'Well, you could get the court's permission to marry.'

'No. That wouldn't be possible.'

I frown. 'Why on earth not? What kind of scoundrel is he?'

She shakes her head again. 'I can't tell you.'

I lean forward. 'Why not?'

'He made me promise not to.'

'He made you promise? But why? Things like this happen. Did he make you promise not to tell, because he was already married to someone?'

She guffaws at the suggestion, and her reaction makes me think. 'Married? Hardly. Although…' She draws back. 'I can't tell you anything more.'

'You know, Bernadette, that I'm a policeman, and you know you have to answer every question a policeman asks you, because if you don't, you'll go straight to gaol. You know that, don't you?' I neglect to mention her right to remain silent at this point.

She jumps in her seat. 'But I can't! I told you, I promised!'

'But those promises don't mean a thing in the eyes of the law.'

'Yes, but they do in the eyes of God!' She begins to weep. 'I can't tell you or I'll be damned to hell! He said so.'

'Who said so?' I probe. 'Surely you know that's not true.'

'But it is true! Father Donnelly said so.' She gasps and bites her lip.

In her reaction, I understand more than she could ever tell me. Quietly, I say, 'I'm going to ask you one more question, Bernadette, and you mustn't lie. You haven't betrayed a promise, but, if what I ask you now is true, you must tell me. You must tell me because what's been done to you is a very bad thing. You are as innocent as a newborn, I see that. The sin is in other people. The sin is not with you.'

She looks relieved, as if those simple words have lifted an enormous weight from her.

I continue, 'God expects a lot from each one of us, but he expects even more from his priests. My question to you is this: is Father Donnelly the father of your baby?'

Her lips tremble and I know I've hit the mark.

'Now, your soul is safe; you haven't betrayed a promise. Is he the father of your baby, Bernadette?'

She wipes her eyes and drops her chin. Quietly she answers, 'Yes.'

CHAPTER TWENTY-SEVEN

I'm still reeling from Bernadette's revelation, even though I'm not totally surprised by it. There's always been something oily about Father Donnelly; he's always been a bit too critical of others, too reluctant to humble himself, and too pious by half. To be honest, I never liked the man, even if I tried very hard to respect the man of God.

I have to put what she's told me aside for the moment, and get on with business. I unlock the next cell. Sharman's still nursing a few bruises, but he's settled down. I'm ready to interview him and I know exactly what I want to ask. He slumps in the chair with a sneer on his face, like he's been here so often, it holds neither mystery nor fear for him.

And we're off…

But things don't go quite as smoothly with Tommy Sharman. Or as predictably. He shuts me down after the first few questions.

'Where were you on Thursday the third?'

'Why? What am I meant to have done on Thursday the third?'

'Never mind. Answer the question. Where were you on Thursday the third?'

'I was at work.'

'Were you?'

'Yep.'

'Where at work?'

'At the Swing Time.'

'All day and all night?'

'All day and all night.'

'I don't suppose anyone saw you. I mean, other than the Diamond Dolls and the usual suspects.'

'Don't know what you mean by the usual suspects,' he smirks, 'but it just so happens that Colonel Reynolds was there. We were having a problem with the owner, so, since the US Government's funding the bloody dance hall, he stepped in to sort it out. He was there a lot of the day, and all of the night, right until we closed in the early hours of the morning. He'll vouch for me.'

'Colonel Reynolds?'

'Yep.'

'Colonel Reynolds?'

'Is there an echo in here? Colonel Reynolds. You can ask him yourself.'

'I will.'

I question him about Maurie and Kate Pilcher, and he swears he's never heard of either of them. He's clueless about Mrs Singleton's line of business, since he's only there as a bookkeeper (as a favour) once a week to work out the *therapists'* pay, and we just happened to stumble in on payday. I tell him that I'll let him go once his alibi for the third's confirmed, but he'd be wise to stick around anyway, because, if he is telling me the truth, he may be needed to help poor Mrs Singleton out. He thinks I'm stupid. I know he's on a nice little earner that he's not about to walk away from any time soon. Besides, I have other irons in the fire as far as Tommy Sharman's concerned.

I get straight on the blower, first to Colonel Reynolds and then to Inspector Bower, but they've both stepped out for a while, so I leave messages for them to phone me urgently. And then I hang around like a bad smell waiting for their calls.

At about seven in the evening, Colonel Reynolds's aide rings me back. The colonel's in Brisbane on crucial business, far too crucial for him to bother about me or my backwater investigation. He'll call me back when he has time. I can only emphasise its importance to her. She says she understands.

So, it seems Sharman's staying put for the moment.

About ten minutes later, Inspector Bower calls. I ask him whether he can check with the New South Wales State Police about any outstanding warrants for Sharman. I give him a description, and tell him that there have been a few photographs of him and his dolls in *The North Star* from time to time. He might want to compare the images.

'I'll do that and get back to you, Jack.'

'Thanks, Inspector, I appreciate it. But that's not all.'

I can hear his foot tapping. It's late. We both want to go home.

'What is it?' he asks impatiently. 'Can't it wait?'

'I suppose it's not urgent. Shall I call you in the morning? There's something I need to run past you.'

He's already detached, thinking of something else. 'Right,' he replies. 'Good night, Jack. I'll speak to you first thing tomorrow.'

CHAPTER TWENTY-EIGHT

What happens next brings me about as close as I've ever been to tossing the whole lot in. If it wasn't for Gracie and the boy, I'd walk out of here and never look back.

I telephone the inspector in the morning and start telling him about the conversation I've had about Father Donnelly. I don't mention Bernadette by name, or that the girl I'm talking about is Mabelle's mother.

There's a long silence at the other end of the line.

'Inspector? You still there?'

'Yes, Jack,' he croaks. 'What is this nonsense about?'

I start again from the beginning, but he interrupts me.

'Yes, yes,' he says, 'I heard you the first time, but this isn't our business. It's a church matter.'

'I don't see it that way. Father Donnelly's subject to the same laws as the rest of us.'

I don't think you understand…' he begins.

I continue, 'I'm thinking that I should bring him in. The way I figure it, the girl was under the age of consent at the time, and he's committed carnal knowledge, Inspector. That's a very serious crime.'

'Yes, Jack, of course it is. But this is a very sensitive matter. We can't just go arresting a priest on some girl's say-so. Especially one with doubtful morals.'

I'm startled. I'm not above adding seasoning to the mix. 'It's more than just her say-so. He was seen.' Of course, I'm lying, but I can be pretty convincing. 'By a parishioner. Someone known to have impeccable morals and a staunch Catholic. A keeper of the law, you might say.'

'What?'

I can hear the blood draining from his face. There's a long pause at the other end, so long in fact, that I'm starting to wonder if the inspector's keeled over.

Finally he says, 'Listen to me, Jack, you don't want to get mixed up in these things. I'll take over from here. You post me what you have, and I'll make sure it's dealt with in the proper manner through the proper channels.'

I don't like being talked down to. 'We've been friends a long time, Inspector, and not once have I doubted you. I've always respected you as a mate and as my superior...'

'You saying you're doubting me now, Jack? If so, I want to know. I have to know if there's a problem here.' He huffs. 'I know how you've always felt about Father Donnelly. It worries me that you're turning it into your mission to wreak revenge on him. You've been a policeman long enough to understand why you should never get involved in the lives of the victims or of the criminals. How do you know that any of what she's told you is true? And even if it is, there's a good chance that the girl led him on. They can be shameful little temptresses when they want to be.'

I shake my head to clear the confusion. 'As you say, I've been a policeman a long time, long enough to know not to get involved in the lives of others, but I've also been a policeman long enough to recognise when someone's telling me the truth. Father Donnelly's a priest and he's an adult. He needs to be called to account. You can't blame the child for his misdeeds.'

'I'll say this once more, Jack. Let it go. I'll look into it and then I'll do whatever needs to be done. You have to let this one go. That's an order.'

I hang up the phone. I'm seething. If she were my child, I'd go straight over to the presbytery and cut off both of the Father's knackers. I would have never disowned her and tossed her in the street to fend for herself, as if she was the wrongdoer.

I send the constables off to run errands before I take Bernadette out of the cell. The makeup she was wearing has smeared all over her face, and she looks a mess. I bring her a washcloth and a bowl of water and she tidies herself up until she looks like a decent young woman again.

I lead her outside, open the car door and she climbs in slowly. I can tell from her eyes, she's frightened. 'What's going to happen to me now?' she asks shakily, as I sit next to her and start the engine.

'I'm going to drive you to the station and buy you a ticket to Townsville.'

She shivers, even though the sun's pouring through the windscreen.

I resume, 'You'll take the train and, when you get to Townsville, you're going to ask for directions to the Australian Women's Army Service. You're going to go there, tell them you're eighteen and you're going to join up.'

'But…' She frowns at me.

'But nothing, Bernadette. You have to promise me that you'll do exactly as I say, or I'll take you back inside and charge you with a number of offences, the least of which will be prostitution. You'll go to gaol for a long time, and that will be the end of you. On the other hand, if you do exactly as I say, you'll have a chance at a new life. The army will give you a roof over your head, training and a decent wage.'

'But I don't have anything: no clothes, no money, nothing. All I've got is what I'm standing in.'

'All you'll need is what you already have. Here's your letter of introduction and a couple of shillings to buy yourself a meal and a few odds and ends. Once you sign up, they'll give you a uniform.'

'What if they don't believe me?'

'Stick to your guns. You say nothing about your past and no one will be any the wiser.'

She's mulling it over, and there's a sudden lightness to her that I haven't seen before.

'Well?' I prod, 'Is it a deal? Do you promise?'

She settles back into her seat and there's a hint of a smile. 'You really think it's not too late for me to start a new life?'

'Of course not. You and I don't need to tell anyone anything. Not ever. We'll sweep this one under the carpet.'

'Well,' she says at last, 'I guess it's a deal.'

CHAPTER TWENTY-NINE

Kate Pilcher is sitting out on the Rileys' verandah when Mahoney and I get there. She's got a scarf and her sunglasses on, puffing like a chimney and drinking a glass of beer. The Rileys aren't there. She's stolen a private moment, hitched up her skirt and spread her legs, enjoying the warm sunshine and the cool breeze off the creek.

Not very ladylike, I reckon.

She scowls when she sees us and covers up her legs.

'What do you want?' she hisses, taking off her sunglasses and giving me the once-over.

I don't beat about the bush. 'I've come to talk to you, as it happens.'

'I've said all I've got to say to you,' she replies and turns her head away.

'Here's the thing, Mrs Pilcher. Your story doesn't make sense. It never did.'

She shrugs her shoulders. 'Not my fault if you can't understand what I've told you.'

I sit down on the chair next to her and she groans. 'So, let's start again from the beginning, and this time you can try telling me the truth.'

'I'm not saying anything more to you.'

'Right. Well, I could always bring you in…'

She groans again.

I continue, 'So, why don't you tell me all about Tommy Sharman.'

'Who?' she asks coolly, but I can tell from her face I've unsettled her.

'You know exactly who. Tommy Sharman came to see you at your place about a week ago. Now, why did he do that?'

'I don't know what you're talking about. I've never heard of Tommy… What did you say his name was?'

'Sharman. Now, that's odd. He's certainly heard of you.'

Her eyes narrow and she butts out her cigarette and throws it into the garden. 'What of it?'

'I want to know what business you and Maurie have with Tommy Sharman, and why you never mentioned his visit to me.'

'Why should I? Apparently, you know everything. Why don't you tell me?'

'Look. I know Maurie wasn't stabbed after boxing with an Aboriginal man with a scar on his face. I know Tommy Sharman is a white man with scars on his face, who used to be a boxer. I know that he knows you and Maurie, and that he was seen at your place. I know your story has more holes in it than Swiss cheese. I know you're protecting somebody. So why don't you just tell me the truth?'

'I said,' she continues, lighting up another cigarette, 'I've got nothing more to say to you. You want to take me in, then do it.' She puts down the pack. *Lucky Strikes.*

'American cigarettes, huh? A gift from a grateful friend.'

Suddenly she turns deathly pale. I've hit a nerve. I stand up abruptly. 'Right, Mrs Pilcher. I'm sorry to have troubled you.'

'You're leaving?' She's confused.

'You've been most helpful. You've opened up a new line of investigation.'

She mouths a word I can't quite make out, and watches me turn away. I can feel her eyes bore into my back as Mahoney and I leave.

'I don't get it,' he says when we get back to the car.

'I reckon we've been barking up the wrong tree. That path we found at the Pilchers'… I want you to follow it. Find out where it leads to.'

Mahoney scowls at me. He's thinking of the snakes again, no doubt.

'Take Higgins with you, if you like.' I explain, 'I've got a hunch.

After that, I decide to go home for lunch; I haven't done it for a while and the way I figure it, I deserve a proper break every so often.

Mikey's at school, but Gracie's happy to see me. 'I've just made tea,' she says. 'I don't know why, I thought you might come by and I brewed a pot.'

'You're a queer old girl,' I reply and I give her a pat on the bum.

Then I slip a parcel into her hand. She looks at me, puzzled, unwraps it and she's grinning from ear to ear. 'Where on earth did you find these?' she asks me. She holds the stockings up to the beam of sunlight coming through the window, and they're perfect. New. Untouched.

'Oh,' I say, 'they're a gift for you. I might have just mentioned your plight to a certain colonel, and he may have just found them and given them to me to give to you.'

'But two pairs, Jack! I can hardly believe it.'

'They're yours. Just put away the bobby socks and enjoy wearing them.'

She holds them against her cheek. 'I'll have to ring and thank him.'

'No, no, don't do that,' I say. 'Even colonels aren't above protocol. He'd be very put out if you did. He'd probably have to deny everything. I mean, the American officers are free to give out presents whenever they like and to whomever they like, but I know he wouldn't want it getting about that you've got two pairs, and Mrs Jessop, let's say, has received none.'

She mulls it over for a while. 'Alright,' she replies, putting the stockings aside and fixing me a sandwich.

I smile. Even in the very best-run police stations, evidence can get misplaced from time to time.

CHAPTER THIRTY

The boys return in the afternoon, red-faced but otherwise unharmed.

'You'll never guess where the track leads to,' says Mahoney. He's as excited as a young pup.

'And where's that?' I ask.

'The American camp.'

I'm already shaking my head. 'But the American camp's the other side of town…'

He interrupts, 'That's the thing, Sergeant. Not the white camp, the other one.'

'The Negro camp?' I say. I'm thinking it over. 'It leads to the Negro camp? Are you sure?'

Higgins weighs in. 'Yep. Nowhere else. Straight there. Three miles—not a long way for a fit man to walk.'

'We spoke to some of the farmers with land along the creek,' Mahoney adds. 'A black bloke in khakis was seen running along the track, not once or twice, but a number of times, by one of the farmers and his wife. The same bloke every time. Crossing over his land. The farmer—I got his name—reckons he got so sick of seeing him that he took a couple of shots at him the last time, just to scare him off. He's pretty sure he hit the bloke, and he hasn't seen him since. We spoke to the farmer and his wife separately, and they both gave us the same description.'

He flings me his notebook and I try to read it, but his writing is as indecipherable as chicken shit. All I can make out (and only because he's printed it in capitals) is *RUSTY TURNER*.

'Type it up,' I say, tossing it back. 'So, Mrs Pilcher's been keeping company with a Yank soldier.'

'That accounts for the smokes and the stockings, I suppose,' Mahoney continues. 'She must have had some sort of business going on with him.'

I admire his innocence. 'Or something else.'

Higgins guffaws, and I'm about to say what I'm thinking, when the telephone rings.

There's a drawl and a puff, as if the caller's exhaling smoke as he speaks. 'Hello, Jack, long time no hear,' says Colonel Reynolds. 'When are you free to come down and visit us again?'

I reply, 'I've been pretty busy I'm afraid, Colonel, but I'm hoping to catch up with you soon.'

'Fine. That's swell. So, you called me because you had something important to ask me. Something that couldn't wait?'

'That's right.'

I ask him and he confirms that Sharman was at the Swing Time, exactly as he'd said. On the third. Yes, he saw him. Yes, Sharman was there all night. His girls were performing, you see, and Sharman was at the very next table. Bought Sharman and the girls a drink afterwards. No, he wasn't mistaken.

I've got to admit, I'm more than a little disappointed. It would have been nice and neat, if he and Kate Pilcher were in it together. Whatever relationship Sharman has with the Pilchers, as far as him being Maurie Pilcher's murderer, that, it seems, is that. And I can't even prove that his connection with Mrs Singleton goes beyond his role as paymaster.

I tell Colonel Reynolds about the murder, and of Kate Pilcher's possible connection to one of his Negro soldiers. I ask if he'll smooth the waters for me to visit the Negro camp, and he says he will.

'I'll order the MPs to give you their full cooperation. I don't want our niggers fraternising with your gals, and if one of our niggers is responsible for this murder, then he needs to swing for it,' he says.

It's as if we're discussing livestock, not humans. I don't know what to make of it.

I hang up and I'm just about to unlock Sharman's cell and pass on the good news when the telephone rings again. Mahoney calls out, 'It's the inspector for you, Sergeant.'

I put away the key and grab the receiver off him. 'Yes, Inspector?'

'You still got Tommy Sharman in your lock-up?' he asks.

I toss Sharman a glance. He's still there, and looking bloody annoyed. Although, I have to say, from what I've observed that's his usual state. I reply, 'Yes, he's here.'

'Good,' says the inspector, 'you keep him there, until I can send someone over to collect him. You were right about him, Jack. I've been on the blower to Sydney: he's got outstanding warrants for a string of crimes going back more than a decade. Worst of all, after he legged it out of Sydney, he was found guilty of murdering some lowlife in Kings Cross. Tried in his absence and convicted. The boys are coming up from Sydney and they're going to start the extradition process straight away.'

'What do I tell him?'

'Nothing yet. Best he not suspect anything.'

'He's been a bit of a handful. When do you reckon you'll be able to pick him up?'

'Today, I hope. Tomorrow at the latest.'

I'm relieved. I just want to be rid of him.

'You won't credit it,' he adds, 'the bugger's either so arrogant or so foolish, that he's been using his real name all this time.'

'You're joking,' I reply. I toss Sharman another glance. He's settled back on his bed now with his eyes shut, but I recognise the look on his face. Knowing that he's murdered someone, you might expect it to be the look of evil, but it isn't.

What's written on his face is the look of perpetual stupidity.

CHAPTER THIRTY-ONE

Gracie meets me at the front door when I get home. She doesn't usually do that. She's usually too busy cooking tea.

'I thought you'd be home an hour ago,' she says anxiously.

'Important investigation, Gracie. I couldn't get away. What's wrong? Is Mikey all right?'

'He's fine. He's playing cricket with his mates.' She looks around and whispers, 'Father Donnelly is here.'

First I try to hide my shock. Then I try to hide my loathing. 'Father Donnelly? Here? What for?'

'He won't tell me, only that's he needs to talk to you,' she replies. 'He's waiting for you in the lounge room. I gave him a beer.'

I don't relish having to deal with him, but I also know that I'd better get in there before he drinks all my beer.

He stands the minute he sees me, and I find myself reading his face for clues. *Does he know?* He doesn't smile: he looks down his nose, ruddy and stern, but then he always looks like that.

'Ah,' he booms. 'John.'

No one calls me John these days, but I'm glad he does, since it takes away the familiarity of Jack. John Joseph Furey died a long time ago. John Joseph Furey died along with my innocence.

'This is a surprise, Father.' It's not hard for me to call him Father despite all that I know about him, since I hated my own so much.

Gracie brings me a beer and notices that Father Donnelly's is nearly finished. 'Another beer, Father?' she asks and I wish she hadn't. 'Or would you prefer tea?'

'Thank you, my child, another beer would be most welcome. Too much tea gives me indigestion.'

I scowl when I hear *my child*, and I can't help it.

'I thought I should speak to you in person, John,' he continues.

'Do you want to stay for supper, Father Donnelly?' Gracie asks.

'No, no, I have other things to attend to, but thank you for your kind offer, Grace.'

Gracie quickly brings back the beers, and I signal for her to leave with a nod of my head.

He sips his beer and says, 'I hear you've been a very busy man lately,' and I wonder what's coming next, but he adds, 'The Americans have stirred up no end of trouble in our peaceful town.'

My eyebrows shoot up. 'The Americans have? I reckon we've got enough trouble of our own making, without worrying about the Yanks. Once we win a few battles, the Yanks might start heading further north and we can go back to being Wangamba again.' Nothing registers on Donnelly's face. I raise my glass, but not in his direction. 'To victory.'

'To a *Christian* victory. With every one of us doing our bit, may we drive the forces of evil from the world.' He places his glass carefully on the table and puffs himself up. He's about to deliver one of his fire and brimstone sermons. 'My visit is not a social call. I have a matter that I need to discuss with you, John.'

I had a feeling...

'It has been brought to my attention by Miss Percy and other members of our congregation, that that abortionist and destroyer of life—that Abaddon—Miss McCarthy, has returned to Wangamba. I hear that she is killing babies again, and I hear that a poor soul was indeed found dead in the bush. That woman is Satan's handmaiden, and must be stopped.'

So that's why you're here.

'I have talked to her,' I reply. 'Floss McCarthy has only come back here to die. She has a terminal illness. I don't believe she's had the strength to do anything since she arrived back in town.'

'How do you know when she came back?'

'She told me.'

'And you believe her? Such people have no conscience; they do the work of the devil.'

'I believe her. She has no reason to lie. She has cancer and she doesn't have long to live. You just need to take a look at her to know it's true.'

He pauses to drink his beer. 'I think you are a good man, and I think you are a misguided man, because you assume that other people are essentially good, too. This woman should be arrested, before she murders any more babies. As a policeman and a man of faith, that is your duty. Papal law is absolute. It should be held above all other law.'

I reply, 'Well, it's not. Floss McCarthy has a right to live wherever she wants.'

'I know your faith creates conflict within you, between the law you must uphold and the law of your conscience, but, John, you should have never allowed her to operate her evil trade in the first place. If you had imprisoned her back when I first told you to, we would not be having this conversation.'

My mouth feels dry. I take a quick drink of beer. 'I had no evidence she was doing abortions. No one reported any, and the doctor never saw anyone ill from an abortion. I raided the place several times, but there wasn't any evidence and I can't arrest someone just based on suspicions. I have to uphold the law, Father: I am not a vigilante.'

He takes a deep breath. 'I have often wondered if you actually applied yourself to trying to prosecute her, or if you chose to look the other way,'—he pauses—'because of a more personal issue.'

I bristle. 'If you mean that I had an emotional involvement with Floss McCarthy, you are mistaken. I've been a policeman long enough to know I have to remain impartial.'

'I think you know what I am referring to,' he replies coldly. He takes another drink. 'Dorothy.'

'What's this got to do with her?' I snap.

'I have it on good authority that your sister visited Miss McCarthy to terminate two of her pregnancies,' he spits out.

'How can you sit in my house, drink my beer and speak ill of my sister? And how can you share the details of the confessional with me?'

'I would never talk about what someone has told to me in a confession, you should know that,' he replies.

'All I know is, Dorothy went to Floss McCarthy to get advice and that's all. She didn't want to have any more children. She was desperate.'

'The sorry truth is Dorothy damned herself by what she did. Because of her, I believe you protected the abortionist. You acted against the teachings of our Holy Mother Church. It is a sin—as well you know—to prevent a child being conceived. I'm very disappointed with you. It's not too late for you to repent.'

I have faith in God, but I reckon that the church has more to do with man than it has with God. These are man's rules, not God's. The church let down my sister. My mother had to put up with my father bashing her, and the Catholic Church always supported him and never her.

Submit to your husband, Mrs Furey... Hide your bruises, Mrs Furey... Don't upset him, Mrs Furey...

The church said the same bloody thing to my sister.

I say, 'Well, you should know better than to listen to idle gossip. What I knew or didn't know, what I did or didn't do is none of your business.' I drain my glass and slam it down. 'My sister was desperate and her kids starving. Do you know what a woman looks like after she's been beaten? The mongrel broke my sister's jaw once.'

Father Donnelly wipes his mouth with a white silk handkerchief. 'But I endeavour to bring husband and wife together and resolve their differences. Through the church's teachings we can change a man who is lost.'

'No, Father, you and your empty words don't do a bloody thing. You've never been married, yet every day you tell women that marriage is sacred, and that they can't leave their husbands. You tell them that mongrel scum like Tim Cullen can flog them, but they have to stick by their man through thick and bloody thin. They have to bear him children year after year, while he drinks most of his pay away. Dorothy and the kids were starving, Father. No one should starve in this country. Gracie and I did everything we could, but we aren't rolling in money. Where was the Church when the kids were crying with hunger, Father? The food the Church provided was nothing. It was never enough to feed a woman and six children.

'I tried to protect my sister as much as I could. When she finally left him, I told that mongrel husband of hers to stay away from her. I warned him that I would flog the living daylights out of him if he ever laid a hand on her again. He listened all right until you told her she had to have him back and then it started again. I knew he would eventually kill her.'

'But he didn't, did he?' He smirks and it makes me furious.

'She died trying to deliver her seventh baby, a baby she should never have had. If he didn't kill her, then you and the Church did.'

Father Donnelly reels. 'I did nothing of the kind! That is blasphemy! I warn you, John, to recant those words or…'

I'm not beyond trading barbs. 'Speaking of blasphemy and damnation, Father, perhaps you should keep your own house in order. The Church says that priests are meant to be celibate. They are not meant to prey on young girls from the congregation.'

He turns crimson and I think he's about to have a stroke.

'I have something to tell you. You've been seen—how do I say this—having inappropriate relations.'

He rumbles like an erupting volcano. 'How dare you! How dare you!' He has his blood up. As he stands to leave, he lashes out, 'Remember what the Catholic Church has done for you, John Furey! Remember, the miracle that was bestowed on you and Grace in the form of Michael Joseph! Shame on you!'

I feel as if I've been walloped over the head by a rolling pin. 'Well then, God pardon us both, Father. Of the two of us, at least I'm willing to admit that I'm a sinner, and ask for forgiveness. I reckon it's high time you looked at your own shame.'

I don't know how much Gracie's heard, but she looks stunned when Father Donnelly storms out of the lounge room and pushes past her with barely a salutation.

She looks to me for an explanation, but right now I just can't offer her one.

CHAPTER THIRTY-TWO

There's an ink blot on my notepad and I spread it with my pen nib, until it has a head, a body, two arms and two legs. A final stroke, and it's Maurie Pilcher with a knife through the heart.

I'm thinking of heading over to the Negro base today.

The base is remote, and set on the driest, scrubbiest land in the area. You couldn't grow weeds on this land. It's surrounded by a high wire fence, and there are two armed MPs posted out front. They start to grill me about why I'm here, but I mention Colonel Reynolds before they get too far along. I'm glad to see he's done his bit, and my name's listed at the gatehouse. They let me in. As I pass through, I get the impression that it's a prison camp, rather than a vehicle maintenance depot and logistics support base. There are igloo hangars dotted all around me, sitting under clouds of dust.

The Negroes are dressed in khaki fatigues. They're dashing about the camp like worker bees in a hive, busy with their business, not looking left or right. They all have work to do, and there are white officers at every turn to make sure they do it right.

I'm allowed into the post commander's office, once I satisfy the MP at his front door that I have the authority to be there. It's a neat affair—desk, three chairs, drawers, a fan—too hot, too orderly, too boring.

I introduce myself.

Lieutenant Rollins looks like he doesn't want to be here and he quickly tells me that he has applied for a combat role. I don't think I've ever heard a desk jockey say he wants to go into combat: this Yank would have to be the first. I get the lieutenant up to speed, and then I ask if any of his men has been caught absconding from the camp. He looks worried, probably because he doesn't like the fact that one of his men might have murdered a local soldier under his watch. It won't read well on his service record. Not good for his future career, I'd say. I worry that he may not want to cooperate, but he thinks it through for a while and then he orders a lance corporal to bring a private up from the stockade.

Not long after, the lance corporal leads Private Haynes into the office. He's flanked by two MPs, holding shotguns. They aren't taking any chances. If Rusty Turner is right, this bloke doesn't fit the description. Haynes is short and stocky. I don't think he could run like Jesse Owens, even with a tailwind. By the state of his face, the poor bugger looks like someone's worked him over a few times.

They push Haynes up to the lieutenant. He draws himself to his full height, leans forward and eyeballs him. Haynes looks down, but Rollins keeps staring.

'So, boy,' he says at last, 'I hear tell you murdered an Australian soldier in his home. You confess it now, and we'll get the hanging over and done with. Because I'm a God-fearing Christian man, I wouldn't want you to suffer too much.' He sniggers, but Haynes just looks scared out his mind. He tries to speak, but nothing comes out.

'What you say? Speak up, boy,' Rollins hollers into his ear.

One of the MPs plants the stock of his shotgun into Haynes's back. When Haynes yelps and buckles, the other MP pulls him to his feet.

'Please,' Haynes splutters, 'don't hang me, sir. I…I…ain't killed no soldier. No, sir, I just stole a few oranges from the orchard, that's all.'

'I don't believe you, boy!' Rollins shouts back. 'And you know why I don't? Because niggers are compulsive liars, rapists and killers, that's why. Isn't that right?'

'I swear, sir. I swear on the Bible. I swear on my mother, I ain't killed no soldier.'

'How dare you swear on the Bible. I believe you're lying to me. Are you a liar, boy?' barks Rollins.

The MP hits him again, and he whimpers and doubles up in pain.

I know I sometimes go in hard when I'm questioning a suspect, but this is too much. I've had enough. I interrupt. 'This isn't the man I'm looking for. I have a description: the man I'm looking for is tall and thin, and he can run fast. And it is very likely that he has a shotgun wound.'

Rollins looks aghast. I've clearly spoiled his plans for a lynching. 'Are you sure, Sergeant Furey?' he asks.

'Of course I'm bloody sure. I have a murder to solve. Why would I give you the run-around?'

'Private,' Rollins says to one of the MPs, 'check him for shotgun wounds.'

He does. 'None, sir.'

'Are you certain it was one of our niggers and not yours, Sergeant Furey?'

'The man was wearing one of your uniforms. He snagged it when he was leaving the scene.' I add, 'Look, if the man I'm looking for has been wounded, he's going to have to seek medical assistance, isn't he? Gunshot wounds get infected, and he's going to be in considerable pain.'

He nods. He looks over at Haynes with disgust. 'I don't want this nigger stinking up my office any longer. Get him out of here,' he orders.

While I've been out at the camp, the constables have been out by the creek doing a line search. I told them to get as many of the local men as they could find to help them. They're still away when I get back to the station, so I make myself a cup of tea and sit at my desk. I pull open the drawer and take out a small bottle of brandy that has been sitting there for years. It's a hip flask, with only a mouthful taken out of it. It reminds of another time, before I joined the police force, before I met Gracie, the time after the war, when my mind wasn't right. I could have easily got on the grog. If I had, I wouldn't have what I have now. I didn't want to end up like so many veterans, drinking myself to a lonely death.

I put the flask back in the drawer and lock it. Then I drive out to the search area.

There's a half dozen or so men across the creek from the Pilchers' place, sitting around a campfire. The flames dance around a blackened billy, and they're all staring at it with intent. It's clear, even from a distance, that they're tired.

I walk over to them 'Did you find anything?' I ask Higgins.

'Just this. Nothing important.'

He hands me a silver necklace with a small locket hanging off it.

'Where did this come from?' I ask.

'One of the men checked over the spot where we found the dead baby. I think he found it there.' He points to a man handing out cups of tea.

I have a quick word with him, and he confirms the find. I return to Higgins. 'Anything else?'

He shakes his head. 'Kate Pilcher's not around. She must be still at the Riley place,' he replies. 'What about you, Sergeant Furey? You find out anything?'

'Not sure yet,' I reply.

CHAPTER THIRTY-THREE

There's a call for me to come to the hospital. I don't have too many details. All I know is that a woman has been brought there unconscious from her house: a suspected poisoning.

A nurse meets me at the front door and leads me down a corridor to the outpatients' area. She tells me to wait while she gets the doctor. Ten minutes later, Dr McDonald appears from behind the dispensary door. He looks under the weather, as usual.

The Doc doesn't greet me, but leads me into an office and closes the door.

I begin to ask him what happened, when he pulls out a small bottle of scotch and a glass. He pours himself a neat scotch and downs it in one. He offers me a glass and the bottle. 'That warms the cockles of my old heart. Although, not so much my liver.'

I shake my head and return the bottle to him. 'The woman?'

'It's that mousy spinster, Vera Anderson,' he begins. 'Do you know her?'

'Yes, of course, the council clerk. What of her?'

'Parents found her collapsed in her room. They think she may have taken poison.'

'Did she try to commit suicide?'

'Not sure. Her parents tell me she's been unhappy of late.'

'And what did she tell you?'

'She's drifting in and out of consciousness.' He pours himself another scotch. 'I can't get much sense out of her. I don't think it's poisoning that's caused it. It looks to me like she's had an abortion that's gone wrong. I'm not sure if she did it herself, or if she was helped. If someone else was involved, it was nothing short of butchery. She's turning septic.'

'Oh.' I know enough to realise that it's a death sentence, without possibility of remission. I don't need this.

The Doc continues, 'She's developed a severe infection. There is a new drug, penicillin, which might save her but it's not available to us mere mortals. It's only available to the military, so I can't obtain any.' He sighs. 'There's not a lot we can do. It's all in the lap of the gods now.'

I enter Vera's room. A nurse bends over her, fiddling with a drip. Her parents stand by her bed, praying. I introduce myself and her father shakes my hand. His face is drawn. I ask if she said anything to them. He says no, and cries.

Vera's eyes are dark holes in an ashen face. She looks at the ceiling, trembling and muttering. I ask her parents, very gently, if they wouldn't mind stepping outside for a bit. I need to see if I can work out what's gone on here.

I sit by her bed and lean in. 'Vera, can you hear me?' I whisper. 'It's Sergeant Furey. Can you tell me what happened?'

She replies, but I can't understand a word, so I repeat my question while the nurse watches me and shakes her head. This time, I add, 'The doctor says you've had an abortion, Vera. Can you tell me who did this to you?'

'Vera!' she cries out suddenly, 'I'm Vera.'

'I know you are,' I reply, 'and you work at the shire council.'

Her brow creases. She's trying hard to remember. 'Shire.'

'You had an abortion, but things went wrong.'

It exhausts her to speak. 'Wally loves Vera.'

'Wally?'

'Wally loves Vera. On a tree. Forever.'

'Is Wally your boyfriend?'

She sighs. 'Going away.'

'An American?' I ask.

She groans this time. 'Yes. Don't go away. The baby?'

'So, is that why you had an abortion?'

Her eyes fix on me. 'Yes. Can't have it.'

'Did someone help you?'

'No, can't say.'

'Who helped you, Vera?'

'Please. Don't ask.'

'A woman helped you?' I probe. 'Was it someone in Wangamba?'

After a while, a single tear runs down her cheek. She answers, 'Floss.' She's sobbing, 'Killed my baby. Killed me.'

The nurse shoots me a look of surprise.

'Floss McCarthy did an abortion on you?' I want to make sure.

She's writhing again. 'Yes, yes!'

'You'll have to leave it there, Sergeant Furey, she's done her best. No point pressing her further: she's too distressed,' the nurse says. She takes me aside. 'I know you've got to do your job, but Floss McCarthy was a good nurse, you know. She just lost her way. Pity...'

I go outside, and nod at her parents since I really don't know what to tell them. Then I walk into the Doc's office. He's having a nap in his chair. The bottle of whisky is almost empty.

He wakes when he hears me. 'Were you able to get any sense out of her?' he slurs, reaching for the scotch bottle and pouring what's left into his glass. He smiles at my disapproval. 'Makes my senses sharper.'

'She said Floss McCarthy performed the abortion,' I tell him.

'Really? I thought Sister McCarthy was more skilled than that. She's slipped.'

'You've seen her handiwork before?'

He fixes a bloodshot eye on me and says, 'You are having a little joke with me, aren't you? You knew, of course. Floss McCarthy was pretty competent; she had a good teacher. Not that I want to speak ill of the long departed.'

'Doctor Hav—'

'Hush.'

Doctor Havelock. The local doctor before Doc McDonald, dedicated and sober, he left town under mysterious circumstances around the same time the moral assembly ran Floss out of it. Rumours swirled around Wangamba that Floss and Havelock were lovers. I heard he died a few years later in a car accident with his wife.

I observe, 'I'm surprised she's doing them. She's pretty sick she said she only came back here to die.'

'Sister McCarthy was always devoted to dispatching unwanted babies and pregnancies for the greater good. In the end, I think it sent her a little mad. Idealism does that to you. You know, she did have her supporters, and a fair few of them were even Catholics. It's amazing what people tell you in your surgery. Far better than any confessional box.' The Doc laughs before having another sip. 'Less judgement in the surgery. I suppose Father Donnelly would have excommunicated them on the spot. No disrespect, but Catholicism seems rather odd to a pagan like me. Why have tortured, unfed and unwanted children running around, when medicine can readily provide a solution?'

'Floss McCarthy was probably the best midwife this town's ever had. She delivered our son.' I huff. 'She's broken the law, and that's that.' I open the office door. 'By the way, Doc, you're not driving home tonight, are you?'

'I thought you'd ask me that. Of course not,' he replies. 'I'm going to be staying here in a vain attempt to pull this girl through.'

'Well, don't get too drunk while you're trying to save her,' I return.

'If you must know, I'm never ever really sober, Sergeant Furey. I wouldn't know what sobriety is.'

I leave the Doc and step outside, not knowing what I'm going to do with all of this. The moon's up and there's a chill in the air. The town's so quiet you could hear a pin drop. The aircraft don't fly at night, so the peace comes as a surprise after the din of the day. It's a welcome relief. *Peace.* Now that's a strange concept since, around here, no one really knows going on with the war, anyway. Not even me. Last time I listened to the radio, the Japs were getting a hiding in New Guinea.

Or so they said.

CHAPTER THIRTY-FOUR

Gracie isn't too happy with me when I get home. She heard something of my chat with Father Donnelly, and she thinks I've committed a major sin. I ask her for forgiveness, but she's still cranky with me when we go to bed. We've hardly ever taken an argument to bed.

That's all I need at the moment: a priest causing marital friction between Gracie and me.

I head out early the next morning, after a cup of tea I've had to brew for myself.

Grace still isn't talking to me.

The boys are at the station when I get there. Another cup of tea and a half hour later, I'm knocking on Floss's door. Her friend answers and introduces herself as Dot Bannister. She's not known to me; she's not a local.

'Floss is unwell,' Dot says without a smile. 'She doesn't want to talk to anyone.'

'Well, she doesn't have a choice in the matter. It's either talk to me here, or I take you both in.' I push past Dot.

'No!' she cries, overtaking me and running down the hallway. She stands outside her door, her arms outstretched to stop me entering.

I could shove her away, but I don't want to. 'Miss Bannister, you can't stop this. You'll also be coming down to the station.'

Bloody hell, I thought it was going to be easier than this.

She mulls it over and lets me in. Floss is lying propped up on a pillow in bed. She's pale as a ghost, and by the look of her, she's in a lot of pain. Her eyes are open, but they have the same lifeless look as Vera. She recognises me.

'Floss McCarthy,' I begin, 'What have you done? Do you realise the situation you've put me in? I'm going to have to arrest you for the attempted murder of Vera Anderson, and for performing an illegal abortion. Doc McDonald says she's not expected to live, which means you'll be answering to a charge of murder when she dies. And you've made your friend an accessory to all of this.'

Dot starts to sob, but Floss looks resigned to her fate. She opens her mouth and I interrupt her with a warning. I may need to use what she tells me as evidence.

'I shouldn't have done it,' she replies quietly. 'I wasn't well and Dot couldn't do it. Dot's nursing me, but she's not a nurse, you see.'

'I'm going to have to take you two in,' I reply.

'Of course you do.' Floss grimaces as she tries to move. 'The girl was desperate when she turned up the other night. She said her parents would kick her out if they found out.'

'Can't you leave Floss alone,' Dot pleads, 'and let her die in peace? Just arrest me.'

'Don't be stupid,' Floss says. 'You didn't have anything to do with it. You didn't even know what I was up to.' She turns to me. 'All right, arrest me.' She pats Dot on the hand. 'Let Sergeant Furey do his job. He has to follow the law. For what it's worth.'

'Well, you'll need to get an ambulance for Floss,' say Dot.

'I'll be right, Dot,' she interrupts. 'Just help get me dressed, give me a good swig of morphine, and I'll be able to walk to the car. Can I come home after I give my statement? I don't have the energy to take off, and Dot won't be leaving my side.'

I look at them. 'You'll be bailed on your own undertaking.'

Dot pours the morphine into a medicine cup for Floss to drink. She holds it as Floss tips it into her mouth, grimacing at its bitterness.

'It's awful, but it dulls the pain for a little while,' she says.

I watch the pain on Floss's face fade a little. Her nightgown climbs up her thighs, as she works her legs around.

'I'll be outside,' I state.

'No, wait,' she says, tugging at the blankets, 'I'm far too buggered for false modesty. I heard about the baby you found at the creek.'

Her words stop me in my tracks. 'Do you know something about it? Were you involved?'

'I wasn't involved, I swear,' she replies, 'but a woman knocked on my door one night wanting an abortion. It wasn't long after I came back here. She seemed pretty desperate. I thought there might be a connection between her and the baby, and I always meant to call you. But how could I?'

'Why do you think there's a connection?' I ask.

'Well, it wasn't too long after her visit that you found the baby. Things decompose quickly, out in the bush.'

'Did you see her? Can you describe her to me?'

'She had a scarf tied around her head and sunglasses on, like a film star, even though it was dark. I tried to turn the outside light on, but she wouldn't let me. Dot didn't see her; she was cooking dinner.'

'What about a description, Floss?'

'Well, she was average height, slender, probably in her late twenties. She spoke low, but she still sounded rough. You know, not educated.'

'Did you offer to do the abortion?'

'I thought about it but I told her I wasn't doing that anymore. I was too ill. Maybe I should have told Vera Anderson the same thing.'

'Could you tell she was pregnant?'

'No, I couldn't tell; it was dark and she was wearing a coat. She reckons the baby was twenty weeks' old,' she replies. 'Far too late, in my book.'

'And?'

'Anyway, she left when I said I wouldn't do it.'

'Did she walk or drive to your place?'

'There weren't any cars outside the house, but I watched her run down the street and get into an old utility.'

'Was it a military vehicle? Did you see a registration?'

'No, it looked like a farm utility.' She adds, 'Even if I'd tried, it was too dark. Now, I have to get dressed. You wouldn't want me coming to the station wearing my nightdress, would you?'

I close the door and step outside. I check my watch and wait for her and Dot to get ready. When a half hour passes, I start to worry. I know she's sick, I know she might like to look her best, but I didn't think it would take half this long for her to dress.

I'm pacing the hallway when I hear a heavy thump from inside the room. It makes the wall shudder. My immediate thought is that Floss has fallen against it. I rush to her door, but it's locked. I call out, but there is no reply. I thrust against the door until the lock gives way, and I stumble inside.

It takes me a while to figure out what's happened.

Bloody hell!

Floss is back in her bed, still in her nightgown, propped up by two pillows and she's leaning slightly to one side. Her eyes are closed now, and she looks at peace with the world. There's no pain on her face. Except for the needle attached to a syringe sticking out of her chest, I'd have sworn she was asleep. Blood's trickled out of her chest all over the bedclothes. I pick up a towel hanging over the chair and cover her chest with it, to soak up the blood.

I check her and she's undeniably dead. I get up and look around the room.

Dot's lying on her back, her feet touching the wall opposite the bed. She has what's left of a broken glass syringe and a needle sticking out of her chest, just the same as Floss's. She's not breathing, and there's no pulse. There are bits of glass on the skirting board, and empty vials of morphine next to a folded piece of paper on the bedside table. I can only think that Dot must have injected Floss first, and then held a syringe against her own chest, and fallen against the wall.

Morphine to the heart, instantaneously deadly.

All I can do now is ring the ambulance, and wait around. I find the phone in the lounge room, make the call and return to the bedroom. I pick up the piece of paper and unfold it.

Dear Sergeant Furey, Floss wrote, *I'm sorry you had to come here today. Dot and I planned this for a while, but your visit set the date. I think you understood what we were trying to do for these desperate women, me and Dr Havelock. I'm sorry about Vera. Except this one time, I always used proper, sterilised equipment and the correct procedure. The women were my patients and they needed my help. Without me, some of them would have died like your sister did. I'm glad I don't have to live any longer in this world. I'm now free from the judgement and punishment. I just want to let you know I did all of this with good intentions...*

By the time I've finished rereading it, the ambulance has arrived. I fold up the letter and put it in my pocket. As they wheel out the covered bodies, I feel like something more than just a strong cup of tea.

I hang about the house for another hour, scratching around for anything that might be a clue to the women who took advantage of Floss's services. Better I find such things than anyone else. I'm putting what I find into the car, when I spot a familiar face standing with a small group of women across the street. It didn't take her long to get wind of what's happened.

The old witch has a better espionage set-up than the Gestapo.

She heads over to me. I really don't want to deal with the old busybody right now, so I jump in the car and turn it over, hoping I can get away before she arrives, but the old Austin stalls. She's peering in and tapping on the window, as I make a second attempt to start the car. It coughs.

I take a deep breath and slowly open the window.

She pokes her head in. 'God's justice was done here today: those sinners will no longer be doing the devil's work in this good Christian town,' she announces. She's full of her usual fervour.

'I can't comment on any of this, Miss Percy, it's an ongoing police investigation.'

She twists her mouth. 'Sergeant Furey, if you had only done your Christian duty and arrested her all those years ago, this wouldn't have happened. God stepped in while the police didn't. Such is God's rule. This will leave a dark stain on this town for many years.'

'I'm sure the town will eventually deal with it. Why don't you look at what's staring you in the face, and you might uncover a worse sinner. Now, please let me go, I have important business back at the station.' I turn the car over. It starts this time, thank God.

She screeches, 'She was a murderer, plain and simple. God has punished her and sent her straight to hell!'

I wind up the window and, in my eagerness to get out of here, I spin the car wheels, unintentionally spraying gravel all over Maud Percy's legs.

CHAPTER THIRTY-FIVE

I drive past the hospital on my way home to check on Vera Anderson. She's still hanging on. Apparently, she's conscious now and her temperature's come down a little. Her parents have never left her side.

Doc McDonald spots me as I'm just about to leave, and he comes over. 'How on earth did you do it?' he asks.

'Do what?' I reply.

'You know exactly what I'm talking about. You hadn't left an hour when I got a special delivery from the US Army. Penicillin. You must have sold your soul to the devil to get it, as I figure it.'

I wink at the Doc. 'You just do your job, and I'll do mine.'

'But how—' he begins.

'Let's just say, I know a man,' I reply.

Late in the afternoon, I find Mikey sitting on the front stairs looking unhappy.

'What's wrong, mate? Bad day at school?' I ask, putting my arm around his shoulders and giving them a squeeze.

He resists me. He never does that. 'Mum's really unhappy. She's been crying a lot,' he replies. 'She says we won't be able to go to church anymore, and it's your fault.'

'What are you talking about? Why did she say that?'

He shrugs his shoulders. 'Dunno. That's what she said, Dad.'

I look around. 'Where is she?'

'She locked herself in the bedroom.'

I pat Mikey on the head and he pulls a face.

'Does that mean I won't be able to go to the same school anymore?' he whines. 'I don't want to go to the state school. I'll miss my mates.'

'Of course not,' I reply. 'You'll still be going to the same old school tomorrow and the day after.'

He balances his elbows on his knees and puts his head in his hands. 'I hope so, Dad.'

'Now, you stay here, while I go and talk to your mother.'

I sneak through the house and try the bedroom door, but it's locked. Gracie's never locked the door on me. I call out, 'Please open, the door, Gracie, I need to know why you're upset.'

She doesn't answer. I knock and call out again, only louder this time.

Again, she doesn't answer. After everything I've been through lately, it unsettles me. I'm concerned she's been taken ill. 'If you don't open up, I'll have to force my way in, Gracie. Please open the door now, I'm really worried.'

I hear the shuffle of feet, and the door creaks. She stands there, her eyes red from crying, her skirt crumpled and her hair untidy.

'What's this about, Gracie?' I edge through the gap and try to hug her, but she slaps my arm and wriggles free. She tries to close the door but she's no match for me. 'We need to talk, please don't push me away.'

She sighs and steps back. 'All right,' she replies. Her face drops and she retreats into the bedroom. 'I guess I ought to hear your side of it.'

I close the door behind me. 'I hate to see you upset like this, darl,' I begin.

She sits on the bed and her eyes track my every move. I try to sit next to her. She moves away. 'Why didn't you tell me?' she says.

'About what?'

'Maud Percy told me that you were the one protecting that

McCarthy woman. She told me you knew what she was doing, and you did nothing about it. That makes you the same as her.'

I feel like punching the wall. That stupid old bitch should keep her nose out of our business.

'She came by here about an hour ago, to tell me that Sister McCarthy and her friend just killed themselves. There's a special place in hell reserved for people like them, and I can't watch you damning yourself alongside them.'

'Please, Gracie, I don't want to go into the details of what happened,' I reply. 'They're dead and that's that.'

'I know you never talk much about your work, Jack, but you should have told me about her. You know our faith condemns birth control and abortion. You should have talked to me and Father Donnelly about it. We could have helped you deal with it better. I think your judgement has been clouded by what happened to your sister.'

As much as I love her, her words rile me. 'My judgement was never clouded. I know the Church's view on such things. It had nothing to do with Catholicism, it had to do with…well, never mind. Anyway, what happened was my sister's choice. I didn't know she'd gone to see Floss until she was dying. She'd never shared that with me before then, and I never agreed with it. I've always upheld the law and, of course I would have arrested Floss McCarthy, if I could have found any evidence.'

'Maud Percy said you tipped her off before the raids.'

I take a deep breath. 'Maud Percy is a vindictive old woman who's telling you lies, Gracie.'

'But you can't say that about her, Jack; she's one of the pillars of the Church in this town.'

'She's a bloody hypocrite is what she is,' I shout, 'and she has no right to make up stories about me!'

Grace's eyes widen. 'Don't you raise your voice at me!' she snaps back. 'I won't be spoken to like that!'

I've taken out my anger on the one person who doesn't deserve it. 'I'm sorry,' I reply, 'I've got a lot on my plate at the moment, and I don't need her making up tales about me. I've done everything to protect the people of this town. I don't need her running about, destroying my good reputation. How can she call herself a Christian?' I sit beside Gracie and it seems I'm forgiven. She melts into my arms.

Quietly, she says, 'You know, you've never raised your voice to me before.'

I feel awful. 'And I never will again. I'm sorry, love. Just to set the record straight, while he was here, Dr Havelock was Sister McCarthy's eyes and ears, not me.'

She sits upright and puts her hand to her mouth.

'He always knew when we were going to raid her house, because he worked closely with us. Old Sergeant Thompson used to tip him off. Havelock would have known everything we were doing.'

'Please, won't you go and tell Father Donnelly that? It might redeem you in his eyes.'

In that moment, I want to tell her everything I know about Father Donnelly, about Bernadette Douglas, about the Pilchers and Mrs Singleton, but I know that unburdening myself would only place the burden on her, so I stay quiet.

That night, sleeping alongside my Gracie and warm in her embrace, I dream of children and women fighting beside me in the trenches.

I'm having another one of my bloody nightmares.

CHAPTER THIRTY-SIX

We head off to church on Sunday, hoping that somehow things may have blown over. Even as we walk through the front gate of the church, all eyes are upon us. We hear the murmurs as we pass by. I say hello to several people, but no one replies.

'Word has spread,' Gracie whispers to me.

'Be strong,' I say to her. 'We have a right to be here.'

Mikey asks me, 'Why are they all staring at us, Dad?'

'They're happy to see us,' I reply.

We go inside and sit in our usual pew, three rows back on the right. Everyone files in behind us, but no one sits in our pew. I look at Gracie and notice she has tears in her eyes.

'We're not leaving, Gracie,' I whisper to her.

With that, Father Donnelly comes out and the mass begins. I'm struck by how old he suddenly looks. He's a broken man. I hear several people gasp. I stare at him, but he avoids me and never looks at any of us. I glance at Maud Percy who's sitting in her usual perch. She turns away.

Gutless old bitch, I think to myself. *You're not bringing me or my family down.*

Mass proceeds without incident until the sermon. Father Donnelly mounts the pulpit as if he is God looking down on us mortals.

He glares in our direction, although his usually strident voice is now frail. I'm thinking that he'll say something soon, and I brace myself for it. In spite of his appearance, he still manages to puff himself up and launch into a fire-and-brimstone lecture about how those who don't follow the laws of the Church are condemned.

'The weak will be swayed by the evils of the society around them,' he pronounces. He doesn't mention my name: he's staring straight at me so he doesn't need to. Then, to add grist to the mill, he goes on and on about the supremacy of law of the Church above all else, the law of the country included. I'm thinking, he'd be tried for sedition elsewhere. *Countries and governments may fall, but the Church remains.* He adds that those who uphold a country's law, rather than the Church's law, cannot be trusted to be good Catholics. Then he goes on and on about the sanctity of life.

It's just a repeat of what he has already said to me a thousand times before. I stifle a yawn.

The congregation seems to be concentrating on us. I reckon they're placing bets on who's going to crack under the pressure, but I know it won't be me. I hang on to Gracie's hand. Her head drops and a tear escapes. Donnelly's an ogre. Seeing her tears makes me want to go up there and drag him out of the pulpit, and tell the world about his hypocrisy, but I know this congregation has no appetite for the truth. Christianity is about forgiveness and tolerance, not this.

Gracie tugs on my sleeve and tries to stand up, but I pull her down again. I hiss, 'We're not leaving. We've done nothing wrong.'

Donnelly finishes up. He says he'll keep the announcements until the end, and then he prepares the Eucharist. Gracie begs me to leave again, but I refuse again.

Maud Percy's looking at us smugly.

The preparation finishes and the congregation lines up to receive communion. Gracie and Mikey go ahead of me. They receive communion but when I go up to receive the wafer, Donnelly hisses at me to move on. I stand there until he repeats it. Using all of my strength not to explode, I cross myself and say *Amen*, before I return to my seat. I can hear the sniggering as I pass by.

Everyone settles back into their pews and Donnelly resumes his spot at the lectern. He apparently hasn't finished with us yet, and I wonder what's still to come.

He clears his throat. 'The ladies have organised a cake stall to raise funds so we can send parcels to our boys overseas. It's to be held in a fortnight.'

Hardly earth-shattering, but Gracie's miffed that she wasn't asked.

He adjusts his spectacles. 'I have news to share with you,' he begins, 'the most wonderful news which, I know, many of you will find uplifting.' He clears his throat again. 'I met with the Bishop last week, and we had a very long discussion. He wanted to pass on his delight with the progress that I, as your priest, and you, as my congregation, have made over the ten years that I have led this parish and tended to your pastoral care. Just as the Lord was to his disciples, I am your good and loving shepherd.'

I look about at the faces that surround us. He's got that right: they're a flock of sheep. I don't think much of sheep.

'My meeting with the Bishop was most illuminating. He told me of the exciting opportunity he had planned for me. Sadly, it is an opportunity I shall be unable to share with you good folk of Wangamba. Like our Lord's ascension on high, I am unable to take you with me. Where I go, you may not follow.

'The Bishop has placed a challenge before me, unequal to any that has gone before, to minister to flocks who may not have heard the Word. Like Dr Livingstone on his mission, I am shortly to depart this parish to lead the church in Halls Creek. It is a challenge I look forward to, since the natives who reside there need a firm and steady hand. Such is my reputation, that I alone was candidate for this mission.

'Do not despair, dear folk, at my leaving, but delight in the opportunities that await me, as I myself am delighted. Although, I can only imagine that in evil hearts the exultation at my departure may be great, I warn such people to beware of their transgressions, since the fires of hell are unrelenting.'

I'm sure I hear a snuffle, followed by Maud Percy's voice crying, '*Hear, hear!*'

'Do not be saddened; another priest shall be given to you, to lead you onwards on your journey, which I may not share. I shall think back on my days in this parish with affection. Except for those few (and they know who they are), I bless you and pray for you. For the others, I pray that the scales may soon fall from their eyes. Repent, and the treasures of heaven shall be shared, even with you.'

I can feel their eyes boring holes in my back. *Bloody hypocrites.*

At last he bids us farewell, and urges us to remain steadfast in our faith. 'Till we meet again on earth,' he says, 'or in glorious paradise.'

I swallow a laugh. *Good bloody riddance*, I say to myself.

CHAPTER THIRTY-SEVEN

I open the desk drawer and pull out the silver locket. It's an unremarkable piece—I doubt it's worth very much—and I'd almost forgotten I'd put it there. I need to tie up loose ends, so I've got my work cut out for me today. I've made a list of people for me to visit, to which I add the town's jeweller.

But first I want to have a chinwag about Maurie Pilcher with Dora Green from the pub and two Diggers from his unit who are about to depart for the front again. I've got to get their statements before I take matters any further.

I catch up with the Diggers first thing at the Jezzine Barracks in Townsville. I'm getting a picture of Pilcher from them and, I have to say, it isn't very nice. He wasn't much favoured by his colleagues. He was a vicious, lazy soldier, according to them. They tell me that he had no qualms about killing the enemy; in fact, he got a kick out of it. They reckon he'd have probably turned his rifle against any one of them, if it had suited him. They didn't know he was married: he wasn't much of a talker. They'd got the impression that he'd run away from something back home—a stint in gaol, most likely. They didn't see him again after he'd departed Townsville, and weren't especially surprised he was murdered.

I'm back in Wangamba by lunchtime, and the pub's jumping.

Dora Green's built up quite a sweat pulling pints. The crowd's four deep around her, all pressing against the grimy counter. I take a moment to order a meal and a beer, and find a quiet spot. I'm happy enough to chow down, and wait until things die down a bit.

Once the rush ends, Dora's finally free to talk to me.

She confirms what the stationmaster has already told me: Maurie Pilcher caught the train in, arriving late in the afternoon. She knows because he walked in with a couple of Diggers who happened to mention it to her. He didn't sit with them: he didn't want company. He drank alone in the public bar until they closed up that evening at eight. She remembers because the more he drank, the nastier he became—swearing and whatnot—until she had to get a couple of the boys onto him.

I calculate that, by the time he'd hitched a ride home from the pub and walked the rest of the way, he must have arrived home pretty much around the time he was killed. That means there was no chance he was in bed asleep with his missus, when she claims they were woken up by the intruder.

Next I take the locket up to The Golden Casket on Jennings Street, hoping that Paul Miller, the jeweller, can tell me a bit more about it. He's there tinkering alone in his workshop when I walk in, and the shop's sour with the smell of solder and hot metal.

His eyes light up the moment I hand it over.

'Do you recognise this necklace?' I ask.

He takes out a loupe and studies it. 'Yes, I do. It's one of mine,' he says.

'You certain?'

'I'm certain. I always put my initials on every piece I make.' He shows me the bail and points to a mark with the tip of his tweezers. 'See? Right here.'

I can't see a thing, but I believe him. 'You wouldn't happen to remember who bought it, would you?'

He thinks for a while. 'No, I don't. It might have been my assistant, Faye, who sold it.'

'Could I ask her?'

He shakes his head. 'She's left.'

'Well, can you tell me when she'll be back? I could come back in another day.'

'No, no,' he explains, 'she's left my employ. Gone south. I don't know where.'

'Oh.' I can't hide my disappointment. *Another investigation going nowhere.* 'Well, thanks anyway for your cooperation.'

He places the locket and chain in a box for me, and hands it back. I turn on my heel. I'm just about through the door when he calls out to me.

'Hang on a moment; I've just had a thought.'

I return to the counter.

'Just wait here.'

He goes into his workshop and riffles through a box of cards. Eventually he finds what he's looking for. He returns to me, holding a card and looking pretty pleased with himself.

'It was a special piece: the purchaser asked me to personalise it. Here's the card for the locket; the chain is just our usual stock. The locket was done for a Private Pemberton, US Army.' He puts out his hand. 'May I see it again?'

I return the locket to him, and he prises it open. 'There's some hair in it,' he says, 'and—right here—I engraved some initials inside it.'

I ask him to place the hair in an envelope for me, and I take a look at the engraving. Even with my worsening vision I can see clearly some initials he's inscribed inside a heart: *KP L KP.*

CHAPTER THIRTY-EIGHT

On the day that I collected them, I posted the hairs from the Pilchers' pillowcases down to the scientific section in Brisbane for analysis. What I've already learned is that one of the samples I sent them had been heavily bleached. Since it was rather long, they concluded that it most probably came from a woman. Kate Pilcher, no doubt.

I'm just about to send them the hair from the locket. I'm no expert, but it looks like a mix of the same bleached hair and someone else's. It's short and dark, and so was Maurie Pilcher's.

I've just finished sealing the envelope. The phone has been ringing off the hook for most of today.

Mahoney's bellowing from the counter, 'Call for you, Sergeant Furey. It's a Lieutenant Rollins.'

I stand up, stretch myself out, go over and take the phone off him. 'G'day. What can I do for you, Lieutenant?'

Rollins seems to be in a good mood. He says, 'You should come out here. We may have found the man you were looking for.'

I nearly drop the phone. 'I'll be right there.'

The MPs wave me straight through and I head to the admin building. The lance corporal takes me straight to Rollins's office.

He's sitting at his desk, looking pretty happy with himself. He announces, 'There's a soldier in the hospital with buckshot in his leg, just like you said. The wound's old enough to develop a real nasty infection. The medics are digging it out now.'

'Did he come in by himself?' I ask.

He shakes his head. 'The sergeant noticed one of the privates limping on the parade ground this morning. He was in pain, so the sergeant told him to go to the hospital, but he didn't want to. The sergeant changed it to an order, but he still refused to go. So he was forcibly taken there.' He leans back in his seat and grins. 'If you ask me, that boy's sure hiding something.'

'Has he said anything?' I ask.

'Nope, he isn't saying a thing,' he replies. 'The medic says he hasn't even cried out for his momma, despite all the pain. Looks like we'll have to beat the truth out of him after he recuperates.'

'Do you think I could have a talk to him?'

He glances at his watch. 'Well, I figure the medics should have finished up by now. We could head right over to the hospital.'

'Will he be well enough to talk? I mean, what about the anaesthetic?'

Rollins scoffs. 'Anaesthetic? Heck, they only dug a few pellets out of his leg, they didn't amputate it, man. Why would the US Army waste good resources on someone who's only going to be swinging on the end of a rope pretty soon anyway?'

I follow him to the base hospital. Pemberton is asleep, his right leg heavily bandaged and both wrists handcuffed to the sides of the bed. There's a sign above him: *Pte K. Pemberton*. Two MPs sit diagonally at either end.

Rollins's eyes drop, and he screws his face up like he's smelled something bad. 'So, this is your man, Sergeant. The dirty lowdown son of a bitch…'

Pemberton's eyes flutter and then close again.

'He talked yet?' Rollins asks the MPs.

'No sir, he's acting dumb,' one of the MPs replies.

'You tried beating the words out of him?' He shrieks at the sleeping figure, 'How dare you kill a white man, boy? And in his own home, in front of his wife? Who in his right mind would do that? Only a Negro would do such a lowdown, disgusting thing.'

Pemberton's awake. He tries to lift his hands, but they're clamped tight. His eyes circle the room. He's terrified.

I clear my throat. 'Do you think I could have a word with him?' I ask. 'In private?'

'Well, he isn't going anywhere. You could try,' Rollins replies. 'I'll station the MPs right outside the door. Just holler if you need anything, and come by my office once you're finished.'

I watch the MPs follow Rollins out the door and then I draw up a chair by the side of the bed.

'Private Pemberton, I'm Sergeant Furey. I'm from the local police,' I begin. 'Tell me, son, how did you get the gunshot wound?'

No reply.

'Right. So, shall I tell you how? You were shot the other night, crossing through a farmer's orchard, weren't you? You weren't supposed to be there. You'd jumped the fence and got out of here, just like you've done dozens of times before. You've been going back and forward, stealing oranges. Except this time, you were seen and you were shot.'

No reply.

'No point in keeping mute. You can talk to me or Lieutenant Rollins. The difference between me and him is, he's got a bad temper and he'll hurt you. Lucky for you, I don't. All I'm interested in is the truth. You've been jumping the fence to get at some of our nice, juicy oranges?'

I can see he's thinking about things. 'Yes sir,' he replies.

'And that's how you got yourself shot?'

'Yes sir.' He pauses. 'I didn't mean no harm by it.'

'You telling me the truth?'

'Yes sir. I'm telling you the truth, Sergeant. I got shot stealing oranges.'

I stare him down until he blinks. 'Except you weren't stealing oranges, were you? You were stealing something else, something you had even less right to. You were shot coming back from Kate Pilcher's place, weren't you?'

Pemberton's eyes open wide. He's scratching for a reply.

'The game's up, Pemberton,' I say, 'I know what happened and why it happened.'

He pulls at the handcuffs, but there's no give in them.

'It must have been all rosy when you were visiting Kate,' I continue. 'Nice-looking woman keeping you happy in a strange, foreign place. And white, too. I bet that doesn't happen back where you come from. Yes, it was all going well until you got her pregnant. So, she gets rid of the baby and she dumps it in the bush somewhere. Did she tell you?'

He looks dumbfounded. I can't tell if he knew. I suspect he might not have.

'And then on top of that, her husband comes home and he catches you.'

He's thrashing from side to side, to the extent that the restraints and his wounds allow.

'You and she just had yourselves a nice supper of corned beef and cheese, and it got your blood stirring. Suddenly, you've got her on her back on the table and you're having yourself a good time. You want to know how I know all this? You left hairs all over the place, and I found some of her hair all tangled up in a splinter in the middle of the tabletop.'

His mouth drops open.

'Then, Maurie Pilcher arrives home without warning, after doing his duty overseas, and catches you in the kitchen, giving it to his missus. He's angry, and who wouldn't be? There's a fight. It gets out of hand, and you pick up a butcher's knife, and you stab him in the chest, and he dies. That makes you a murderer. You murdered him. You murdered Maurie Pilcher, Private Pemberton.'

'No, no!' he yells. 'I didn't kill no one!'

'Really? Then who did?'

He turns his head away and doesn't say a word.

'What? Are you telling me Maurie Pilcher stabbed himself? Of course he didn't. You stabbed him, Kate Pilcher told me. She's signed a statement saying so. She says you raped her,' I lie. 'You're in big trouble, son. You're going to hang, and no one can help you.'

The MPs have been listening at the door. They poke their heads in. From the looks on their faces, he's in for a rough ride.

'I never raped or killed no one, sir,' he cries over and over, until it grates.

I purse my lips. 'Well, that's not what Kate Pilcher told me. All I can say, is you're really in the stink now.'

CHAPTER THIRTY-NINE

I have to admit that perhaps I went a bit too far when I interviewed Private Pemberton, but since he was lying, I thought, so would I. He's a murderer: of that I'm sure. That means he has no rights, as far as I'm concerned.

You know, in policing, sometimes the end really does justify the means.

The following day, I decide to visit Kate Pilcher once more to see what she has to say about him. If I've read her correctly, she'll happily throw him under a bus just to save herself, and it'll be case solved. I suspect she's as big a maggot as her husband was, and Pemberton's the willing fool. I have to wonder if she didn't set it all up, just to rid herself of her troublesome old man.

Valmay Riley's confirmed that Kate Pilcher's returned to her own home (*at bloody last*), and that's exactly where I find her. As I drive up, I have to say, the house is looking even shabbier than it did the last time I was here. A mop hangs over the broken balustrade by the front steps, with an upturned bucket next to it. At least she's been cleaning.

I rap on the door, but it's already ajar and I can see down the entire length of the house. It smells vaguely of phenol and cigarettes.

'Hello!' I bellow. 'Mrs Pilcher?'

She comes out of one of the rooms, and stands at the end of the hallway, with her hand on her hip.

'You back again?' she mutters as she approaches. 'What do you want now?'

'I want to talk to you,' I reply.

'Yeah? And here's me thinking you dropped in because you were after a word with my husband.' She sniggers. 'Oh, that's right, he's dead. But you can't seem to find the Abo that killed him.' She grunts. 'So, what do you want to talk to me about?'

'I think we may have found your husband's murderer, Mrs Pilcher.'

Her eyebrows shoot up. 'Really? Well then, I suppose you'd better come in,' she says.

I follow her to the kitchen. It's been scrubbed clean and the old table and chairs are gone. She's replaced them with something even worse. She stands near the sink, turns and watches me. I'm revisiting the moment I first walked into the kitchen, but she's emotionless. I find that disturbing.

'Why don't you sit down?' I say to her, pulling out a chair.

'I prefer to stand, actually.' She shakes out a smoke, and lights up. I notice that her hands are trembling again.

I won't sit if she won't. I say to her, 'Why don't you tell me all about Karl Pemberton.'

'What the fuck are you talking about? I only let you in here because you said you'd caught the black Abo bastard that killed my husband.'

'And I still believe I may have found the murderer.' I bite my lip. 'Shall we cut the crap, Kate? You and I both know Maurie Pilcher wasn't killed by an Aboriginal. Maurie wasn't in bed with you, he was at the pub until he walked in here, and found you having intimate relations with your black US serviceman boyfriend. Pemberton's hair and fingerprints are all over this house. You had American cigarettes and stockings stashed in the roof. And to top it off, he was seen coming and going on a regular basis.'

She shrugs her shoulders but offers me no explanation.

'You know what I think? I think you knew Maurie was coming

home that evening, and you lured Pemberton here to murder him. Maurie Pilcher wasn't a nice man; there are warrants for your arrest and his, down south. I know that back in the day, you both ran with Tilly Devine. Did you finally get sick of being Maurie's punching bag?' I ask.

'I dunno what you mean.'

'You know exactly what I mean. And by the way, your old friend, Tommy Sharman, is currently serving time in Long Bay Prison.' I watch her blanch. 'So, don't you be so cocky. I know you used that poor fool Pemberton to rid you of that bastard husband of yours.'

She takes another puff and composes herself. 'I had nothing to do with what happened to Maurie, and you can't prove otherwise.'

'Really? You were in such a hurry to get away from the raping, murdering intruder that you stopped to wash, change out of your bloodied clothes, put on your shoes and tie up your shoelaces. Shame you forgot to wash the blood out of your hair. There's no forced entry, fingerprints on the cups in the sink, a door unlocked and relocked… More bullshit than you'd find in a cattle yard. You want me to go on?'

'Don't you try and stitch me up, you copper mongrel.' She looks away. 'I told you the truth.'

'Exactly which truth was that? The first version of truth? The second version of truth? Which version will I get today?' I glare at her. 'And what about the baby you aborted yourself when Floss McCarthy said she wouldn't help you? Why don't you tell me about that?'

That sends her reeling. She holds onto the back of the chair. 'How dare you!'

'Your boyfriend, Pemberton, spun me an interesting tale when I spoke to him yesterday. Now, I don't much care if you held the knife that killed your husband or he did. You planned it and, for your peace of mind, I reckon you executed it. At very best you'll be convicted as an accomplice. Which means you and Pemberton, you're both murderers. You know what Yanks do to murderers? They hang them.' With as much drama as I can muster, I raise my arm high over my head, open my palm and something drops out. The silver locket dangles, rocking backwards and forwards, suspended from my fingers by its chain.

She puts her cigarette down. Suddenly, even with the back door wide open, there's not enough fresh air in the kitchen to fill her lungs. She's huffing like a steam train.

'I…I…' she begins. Her knees buckle but she still doesn't sit down.

I continue, 'Karl Pemberton loves Kate Pilcher? The lovers' hair intertwined? A dead baby? A dead husband? You really need me to tell you what a jury will make of all that?'

Her face drops. She's already tried bored and angry with me and it hasn't worked, so now she tries a different approach.

She looks away and says, 'I didn't do nothing wrong. I was the victim, here, not Maurie and not Karl. Maurie was cruel, you got that right. And all right, maybe I did think about having an abortion, but I never did, did I? I lost the baby, but that was only because Karl hit me. Turns out that he was almost as cruel to me as Maurie was. The only thing I ever done wrong was go for bad men.'

'So, why don't you tell me what happened then, Kate?'

'I only went with Karl because I was desperate for some stockings and stuff to sell, so I could support myself, that's all. It's hard to live on Army pay, so I let him do whatever he wanted, and he give me nice things in exchange.'

She blinks away tears that never were, and it makes me sick.

'I know I shouldn't of,' she says. 'I'm not proud of myself, you know. I suppose, in his own way, Karl fell in love with me. I never wanted that. Imagine it! Me and a blackfella!' She sniggers. 'Even I've got standards, you know. Well, I never thought he'd fall in love with me, or that I'd get pregnant to him. Me and Maurie together for years and no babies. Me and Karl together for a few days and suddenly… Well, I always wanted a baby, but not this: I never wanted a blackfella's baby.' Steady now, she takes another puff of her cigarette and puts it down again.

'Karl got real angry when he found out I was pregnant, and he accused me of trying to use the baby to make him give me more money, which I never done. Then, one night…he came over and he…he bashed me black and blue, till I dropped it. He killed my baby, not me. I told him then and there to piss off. I never wanted him to darken my door again, but he came back that night Maurie was killed and he raped me. Poor Maurie caught him in the act. He died trying to defend me. Karl stabbed him. He got the knife and he stabbed Maurie. In cold blood.'

She stops again and glares at me, and I feel like I'm a schoolchild again, listening to someone spinning a ridiculous yarn.

'I can't be an accomplice to something I never even saw coming, now can I?' she demands. 'You can see that I had nothing to do with it.'

She's barely finished talking when there's a noise from the backyard, a loud bang followed by some scraping. Our heads turn towards the open door. There's a heavy thump and an unbalanced footfall. I'd assume someone jumped a fence, except that it's coming from the wrong direction.

Kate suddenly looks scared.

I spring up, my fingers touching my truncheon, but I don't clear the chair in front of me, when Pemberton stumbles through the door. His face is drawn with pain.

'Stop there!' I shout, but he doesn't seem to hear me. I hurl myself forward, not really knowing what I'm going to do, but my foot tangles in a broken stretcher running between the legs of the chair, and I fall hard to the floor. There's a searing pain in my ankle.

He's wild—a mess—and his right hand grips his thigh. He blinks until his eyes adjust to the gloom, and then they dart from Kate to me, and back again. He says breathlessly, 'This doesn't involve you, Sergeant. Don't you move another muscle; I don't want to hurt you.'

I start to ask Pemberton how he got out of the hospital, when I notice the handcuff still fastened around one of his wrists. His pyjama sleeve covers most of his left hand, so it takes me a while to realise that he holds a pistol.

He continues, 'I've come to fetch you, Kate.'

Her mouth drops open. 'What?' she mumbles. 'Fetch me where?'

'I've come to take you away, girl. We're leaving this place together, just like I promised you.'

I can tell from her face this wasn't her plan. 'But…' she begins.

'You don't need to bring anything. I've got everything we need: money, this gun, and a Jeep out front. We can run away from here, you and me. We can be together forever. You want that, don't you?'

She lets out a gasp. Quietly, she replies, 'I can't do that, Karl. There's nowhere for us to run to. You know we can't do that.'

I try to interrupt, to ask him to drop the pistol, but he isn't listening. Instead, he waves the pistol around. I can't tell if the safety's on or off. For the first time in my life, I've drawn a blank. I feel every one of my near fifty years, and I can't put any weight on my foot. I know I can't possibly disarm him.

He softens. There are tears in his eyes. 'I loved you, Kate,' he says, 'more than I loved anybody else in this world.'

She frowns and struggles to respond. 'Yes, me too.' She spits out the words like poison.

He doesn't seem to notice. 'You sure you don't want to run away with me?'

'I'm sure.'

'Because I've got to go. I can't turn back after what I've done.' He looks at me. 'This isn't your problem, Sergeant, and the military police, they're gonna be after me soon enough.'

He's right, of course. Desertion's a big deal in war.

He continues, 'I only want one more thing: I want to kiss you just this one last time, Kate, and after that, I'm gonna go.'

She nods. 'This is my home. You go, Karl, you run, but I can't leave.'

The gun slides out of his hand, or he drops it, I don't know which. In spite of everything, he's still strong. He gathers her in his arms and dips her, like a silent movie star, and she's compliant. He's still young, tall and athletic. He leans in towards her, but instead of kissing her, he cradles her head in his arms and buries his nose in her hair. On his face there's a mixture of love and despair. He doesn't say another word. Unexpectedly, he pulls away and his hands glide down her face, squeezing her cheekbones so hard that the flesh bulges. She looks aghast. Her chin now rests in the crook of his arm, her face drenched with his tears. He looks towards the ceiling.

Her lips part but she can't get out the words.

His eyes never leave the ceiling. His hands move quickly, a sharp twist, a flex of his forearm, a crack as loud as the limb of a tree breaking, and Pemberton snaps her neck.

My mind reels as I watch Kate crumble like a rag doll, and her legs twitch. I try to stand up, but the pain's awful and my ankle gives way.

He makes a noise like an injured animal. Turning to me again, he wails, 'It was all lies. I heard what she told you before, and it was all lies, Sergeant. That woman was pure evil, and now I've damned myself to hell. I got no reason to lie to you. You gotta know that she killed her husband, not me. She stuck him with the knife, and I ain't about to hang for something I didn't do.' He's still sobbing as he blindly feels for the pistol.

As his fingers curl around the handle, I say, 'No, Private Pemberton, please wait...she's not...'

He lifts the pistol up and wipes his eyes on his sleeve. 'They'll hang me for being a deserter, or they'll hang me for being black. Either way, I'm a goner. I ain't gonna hang,' he says, staring straight at me.

I'm still thinking about Gracie and the boy, and how they'll cope once I'm gone, when he cocks the pistol and shoots himself in the temple.

CHAPTER FORTY

I don't have much of an appetite for anything for the next few days: I have a body and a soul to heal. Gracie and the boy steer clear of me for a while. They seem to understand.

In my line of work, you soon realise there is no redemption, and no one is saved.

In my position, the only thing you can count on is that there will always be reams of forms to be filled in.

Kate Pilcher's laid to rest, and I'm the only one there. The US Army collects Pemberton's body and he's counted as just another casualty of war. Who's to know, maybe that's exactly what he is.

Gracie's right: what I do isn't about granting absolution. That's someone else's job. The best I can do around here is offer people a little peace of mind, and some very basic justice.

We arrive at church on Sunday, not knowing what to expect. There's a chill in the air and you could cut the atmosphere with a knife. Everyone is avoiding us, yet again. I tell Grace and Mikey to stand tall, walk proudly and look everyone in the eye, and then I hobble over with them to our usual seats.

The congregation's strangely quiet, like it's the first day of school.

The first inkling I get that things might have changed is when Maud Percy arrives late. She's always early. The old biddy settles into her usual spot, eyes dead ahead, avoiding all conversation. She's taking Donnelly's exit pretty hard. She pulls out a handkerchief and dabs her eyes. *Is it possible that she and Father Donnelly... Surely not...* My mind wanders to a place I'd sooner not go, until I quickly rein it back in.

There's a new priest in the sacristy, a Father O'Loughlin. I hear tell that he's a Franciscan, although I don't have much faith that he'll be any bloody different from those who have gone before: hypocrites the lot of them. I start to tell Gracie that, and she hushes me.

In nomine Patris et Filii et Spiritus Sancti. Amen.

So far, there's nothing new. O'Loughlin's younger than I expected, but I'm a cynic. I don't count on much. My optimism's been eroded down to just about nothing by the rub of countless years of bitter experience. We eventually get to the sermon, and my eyes glaze over.

'Today,' he begins, 'marks the start of a new era in my life and hopefully in yours. Our Lord taught us love, forbearance and forgiveness. Judgement and gossip have no place in our church, and from now on, it is not going to be tolerated.'

He speaks of the passing from one generation to the next, and I want to take a sly glance at old Maud Percy. Then we line up to receive the body and blood of Christ. He sees my crutches and comes to me first, and gives me communion without a second thought.

He doesn't have a bloody clue who I am.

At the end of the Mass, he's outside, shaking hands without a smile. He's a sober young thing. As I pass by, he abandons the flock gathered around him, and seeks me out. Gracie looks worried.

'Sergeant Furey,' he says. 'I am very happy to see you here today. How's the leg?'

'Getting better daily,' I reply. I look for clues as to where this is all heading.

'I wanted to let you know that the Archbishop sends you his regards. He asked that I tell you that. He knows the job you've done for Wangamba, and the obstacles you've had to face. Apparently,

Father Donnelly's settling down well in the Territory.' He blinks. 'The Archbishop asked me to tell you to be patient: the winds of change aren't always a tropical cyclone.'

I'm astounded. *I never thought in a million years...* Gracie's pleased as punch. Mikey even grins.

'Well, I don't know what to say,' I begin. And I honestly don't. *The Archbishop?*

The congregation stand open-mouthed, and suddenly I'm back in the fold.

What did I tell you? They're still all bloody sheep.

CHAPTER FORTY-ONE

Nursing home, 1993

So the sun rises on my hundredth birthday and I don't give a shit. It's just another day without my Gracie. I'm fed and watered, dressed in my best suit and Tanya's combing my hair in readiness for the day's celebration. I'd let them know exactly what I think of all the palaver, if I could only find my tongue.

I spend much of the day reminiscing with Viv Morley again, but he reckons he can't stay for the party. He's just popped in for the couple of days he's in town, and now he's off again. He won't say where. We've been practising my talking since he arrived and, you know, I reckon I've improved a lot. He's better than any of those bloody therapists they've made me see over the years.

I might even make a speech today.

Finally it's show time, and Tanya comes to fetch me. I can already hear the music travelling down the corridor and it's bloody Slim Dusty. Did anyone check with me? I may have lived most of my life in the country, but that doesn't mean I like the bloody music.

All the chairs in the lounge are stuck around the walls like spinsters at a ball, but there's a table in the middle set up just for me, with helium balloons tied to it. Most of the residents are wearing silly hats. They'd better not try to put one on my head. The mayor and his wife aren't wearing any, and neither is Shifty Harrison. And neither will I.

Tanya wheels me over to the table. I smack her hand away when she approaches me with the hat, and she understands. Someone turns off Slim and I feel like cheering, but I'd be drowned out by all the whistles and applause. I look around at everyone's faces; these people don't know a thing about me. They're all insufferable bores.

My so-called family's here: my son and his polished-to-within-an-inch-of-her-life wife, their eurotrash children, and their brats, and so on and so forth. They're a pack of arrogant toffs. The mongrels only visit when they hear I'm sick and could die. That's what happens when you raise your only son to be an educated man. Who'd have thought that sweet little Mikey would end up as Michael Furey QC, Supreme Court Judge? The trouble with my son is he became too important, and forgot all about who helped get him there. He married that blonde trophy wife of his (her father was the Australian Consul to some God-forsaken third world backwater), and suddenly we're *persona non grata*. Gracie and I. We worked our fingers to the bone to get him where he was. And his family are insufferable. I'm surprised they're even here.

They think I'm going to leave them everything in my will? Well, I have some bad news for them…

'Happy birthday, Pa,' my son says with a laugh as fake as his wife's tits, 'so good to see you.'

The wife bends over to kiss me, but I splutter and catch her with a little sputum on the cheek, and she nearly vomits. At one hundred, that sort of thing tends to happen. Just ask poor old Tanya.

Shifty Harrison comes over. He pats my hand again. 'It's the least we could do,' he says, although I haven't thanked him. 'You've had a long and momentous life.'

Oily bastard. If I was a young bloke again, I'd give the show-pony the flogging of his life. Tanya wipes my eyes and gives me a hug.

After a bit of shush, the entertainment starts up. Val and her alcoholic husband Ron, well, they're about as entertaining as a dog having a crap on your lawn. If they sing those hillbilly songs and do any of that stupid boot-scooting rubbish, I'm going to deliberately shit myself, just so I can get out of here. *Give me Mario Lanza or Pavarotti any day.*

They start off with 'You are my Sunshine', and the only reason I'm still sitting here is that Gracie liked to sing that song to me. My son looks over and he winks. It's just a coincidence. He couldn't possibly remember that.

Eventually Shifty Harrison carries in a cake. It's nothing short of a joke. It's big and blue and ugly and studded with candles. He starts to light them, but it soon becomes pretty obvious that the cake's about to go up in flames, so he takes most of them off.

I'm one hundred, not five, you idiot.

I blow them out and wish they'd left me alone.

'Do you want a cup of tea?' Tanya asks.

I shake my head.

'I know it's all a little overwhelming for you, Mr Furey,' she says, 'but people really care about you. You have done a lot for Wangamba.'

I really wish they did care, but I know people a bit better than she does. They don't. No one cares about an old man who just sits in a chair most of the day, with only his good and bad thoughts to help him pass the hours, waiting to die. When the highlight of your day is getting showered, or when someone has to wipe your arse, then I think it's time you should be moving on.

Tanya dabs my eyes again and I pretend to smile. I'd love to tell her why I'm really upset. It's not just the party that I've been press-ganged to attend, it's the memories. There are the good ones, like the ones of my lovely wife. But there aren't enough of them. Then there are the other ones, the ones I wish I could forget. Those depression tablets don't do a thing for them, let me tell you.

The dreams always get worse around my birthday.

Shifty Harrison's introduced the mayor and now they're talking about my career like they have a clue, and I'm not in the room. 'What some of you might not know is that, as well as being a decorated war hero, Jack is a Member of the British Empire. He didn't have to wait until today to receive recognition from the Queen. He's also received a Knight's Cross from the Pope… '

Ancient bloody history.

I put out my hand and snatch the microphone off him. I figure it's about time I had my say. The mayor looks taken aback, and he tries to make a joke of it, but I'm deadly serious.

I begin, 'I'd like to say I'm glad to see you all here, except I'm not.' I'm pleased at how well I'm speaking, and how successful Viv's tuition has been. I look around at the crowd and, I have to say, they all look shocked. I continue, 'I really never wanted this…'

Michael's turned white as a sheet. He leaps up and tries to wrestle the microphone away from me. 'No, Father!' he yells. 'Stop!'

I wonder what's got his goat. 'Sit down, young fella,' I growl, 'haven't you had enough public speaking, sitting on the bench for all these years?'

'Stop!'

'What's bloody wrong with them?' I ask Shifty. He looks like he's about to cry.

Around the cheap seats, my fellow inmates are roaring with laughter.

Tanya steps forward and whispers in my ear, 'I know you think you're talking to us, but you're not. All we can hear is gibberish.'

I start up again, this time without the microphone.

'For God's sake, shut up!' Mikey bellows. 'You're an embarrassment to yourself and to us!'

But I continue. Mikey's wife's inconsolable. The TV reporter's having a blast.

Above all the din, I can hear Mikey screeching. 'For fuck's sake, Dad, will you stop saying fuck!'

My mouth drops open. I attempt to talk again but all I can do is dribble. My head feels like lead. *So bloody heavy.* I feel myself slumping forward. Strangely, I don't feel any pain when my head hits the floor. Maybe I'm already dead. *Now's that a darn relief.* I don't have to stay at the birthday party any longer.

Here I come, Gracie.

I don't care about dying one bit. Why should I? I thought I was going to die every day when I was in that awful war, and a fair few times when I was a copper. I'm not afraid. When I glimpse Gracie, there's not a worry in the world. In fact, I've never felt so happy and calm.

She still looks young and beautiful: skin the colour of ripe peaches, huggable curves, rosy lips. I could go on forever about her. She's wearing that dress of hers, the green one, my favourite. It fits her like a glove. I want to hold her again and kiss her from head to foot.

Well, it has been a long time.

I'm happy as the proverbial muddy pig. I hear Shifty's frantic voice calling me. And Tanya's. And even Mikey's. I'd like to tell them all to bugger off, leave me alone. I want to be with my wife. Tanya shakes me. I hear the emergency bell ringing.

After that, I hear Grace's soft, tender voice calling me. 'Come on, Jack, my dear, I've missed you,' she beckons. 'You've mucked around in this place for too long. Come on.'

'I'm glad you're here. my love,' I reply, 'I've been waiting for you to get me for thirty years. Where have you been? Get me out this bloody dump.'

'Just take my hand, Jack.'

She holds my hand and we walk away into the most beautiful sunset I have ever seen.

'Cup of tea, love?' she asks.

'Love one. I bet you haven't forgotten how to make it.'

'I've never forgotten anything about you, especially how you liked your tea,' she replies.

'Same here, love, same here. I've never forgotten a thing about you.'

'Now, let's head home. It's been a long day.'

THE END

www.ingramcontent.com/pod-product-compliance
Lightning Source LLC
Chambersburg PA
CBHW020147120726
47903CB00007B/2441

* 9 7 8 0 6 4 5 0 9 9 1 9 5 *